Praise for

A FIELD GUIDE
to Getting Lost

"A character-driven tale that doesn't skimp on plot. . . . Minor perils and likable characters make for a cozy and enjoyable read."

—*Kirkus Reviews*

"McCullough's fantastic middle grade debut centers on two kids who could not be more different—or so they think. . . . This title is enjoyable and covers topics many children will relate to. . . ."

—*School Library Journal*

"Readers will appreciate the enjoyable narrative about odd ducks finding their flock and learning how to adapt."

—*Bulletin of the Center for Children's Book*

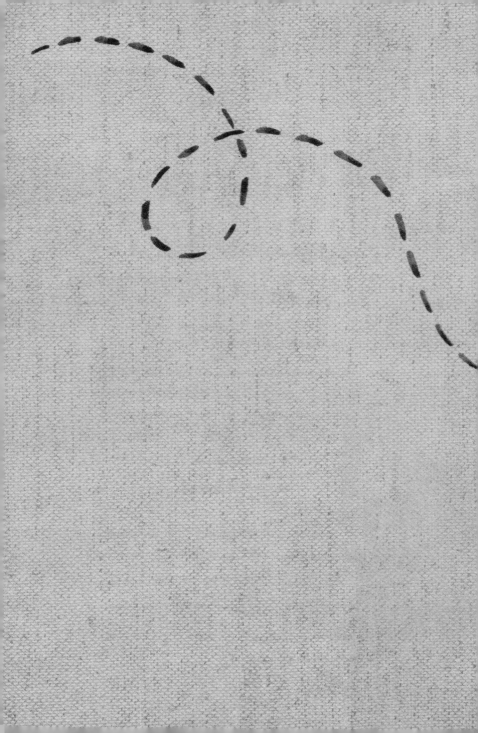

A FIELD GUIDE

TO

Getting Lost

JOY McCULLOUGH

 Atheneum Books for Young Readers
atheneum New York London Toronto Sydney New Delhi

ATHENEUM BOOKS FOR YOUNG READERS
An imprint of Simon & Schuster Children's Publishing Division
1230 Avenue of the Americas, New York, New York 10020
This book is a work of fiction. Any references to historical events, real people, or real places are used fictitiously. Other names, characters, places, and events are products of the author's imagination, and any resemblance to actual events or places or persons, living or dead, is entirely coincidental.
Text © 2020 by Joy McCullough
Cover illustration © 2020 by Isabel Roxas
Cover design by Greg Stadnyk © 2020 by Simon & Schuster, Inc.

For information about special discounts for bulk purchases, please contact Simon & Schuster Special Sales at 1-866-506-1949 or business@simonandschuster.com.
The Simon & Schuster Speakers Bureau can bring authors to your live event. For more information or to book an event, contact the Simon & Schuster Speakers Bureau at 1-866-248-3049 or visit our website at www.simonspeakers.com.
Also available in an Atheneum Books for Young Readers hardcover edition
Interior design by Irene Metaxatos
The text for this book was set in Minion Pro.
Manufactured in the United States of America
0221 OFF
First Atheneum Books for Young Readers paperback edition March 2021
10 9 8 7 6 5 4 3 2 1
The Library of Congress has cataloged the hardcover edition as follows:
Names: McCullough, Joy, author.
Title: A field guide to getting lost / Joy McCullough.
Description: First edition. | New York City : Atheneum Books for Young Readers, [2020] | Audience: Ages 8 Up. | Audience: Grades 2–3. | Summary: Told from two viewpoints, STEM-oriented Sutton and imaginative, artistic Luis, ages nine and ten, must find some common ground when her father and his mother start dating seriously.
Identifiers: LCCN 2019035650 | ISBN 9781534438491 (hardcover) | ISBN 9781534438507 (pbk) | ISBN 9781534438514 (eBook)
Subjects: CYAC: Dating (Social customs)—Fiction. | Single-parent families—Fiction. | Fathers and daughters—Fiction. | Mothers and sons—Fiction.
Classification: LCC PZ7.1.M43412 Fie 2020 | DDC [Fic]—dc23
LC record available at https://lccn.loc.gov/2019035650

For Joaquin—
may you have many adventures
and always find your way home

Sutton

The robot had a mind of its own.

Thankfully, the robot was the size of a golf ball and was not likely to overthrow the human race. At least not anytime soon.

Sutton looked carefully at the code and tried again. But again the little robot refused to turn right when it was supposed to. Coding was always black and white—you wrote the code correctly and your program responded how you expected. Two plus two equaled four. Or, more to Sutton's level, pi equaled 3.14159265359. There was no wiggle room, not like taste in books or music, which her dad was always telling her was subjective. Like that was a good thing.

In her last email, Mom had asked Sutton if she'd managed to get the bot through the maze in under a minute yet. Sutton had been surprised her mom remembered the robot. Even when Mom was in town, Sutton did all her school stuff with her dad. (Which mostly meant he looked over Sutton's proposed research topics and gave them a thumbs-up.) Thrilled by her mom's interest, Sutton had fudged a little and told her the robot had passed the test with flying colors. Which meant she needed to be ready to demonstrate when Mom came home next week.

When the robot refused to make the turn a third time, Sutton shoved her coding book off her desk. Somehow the loud thunk as it hit the ground helped release the tension that had been creeping up her spine. She picked it up and dropped it again.

"Whoa there, pumpkin." Her dad appeared in the doorway, dressed for work—black suit, shiny shoes. "What did that book do to you?"

Sutton frowned. According to their synced calendars, her dad was not supposed to be at the orchestra tonight. "Why are you wearing your blacks? Is there a performance tonight?"

He hovered in the doorway for a second. "Can I come in?"

She nodded, and her dad sat on the end of her bed. "No show tonight. I have a date."

Now her dad was the one refusing to follow the expected route. "A fancy date," she observed.

A smile passed over his face, but he wrestled it back into a serious expression. "Yeah, you know I've been seeing Elizabeth for a while now. I thought it was time we stepped it up from hikes and coffee."

Her father had gone out with Elizabeth seventeen times so far. Five hikes, four coffee shops, two combo hikes/coffee shops, two daytime movies, three evening movies, and miniature golfing. It seemed like their relationship had been stepping up for a while now, but then what did Sutton know about dating?

"We're having dinner at Cielo downtown and then going to the opera. I talked to you about this at breakfast."

This was vaguely familiar. "Was I fully prepared to engage?"

He chuckled. But it wasn't funny. Sutton's dad knew that until she had completed her morning routine—making hot chocolate, watering the apartment's jungle of plants while her apple-cinnamon oatmeal cooked, then eating while she mentally recited the periodic table of elements and the United States presidents in chronological order and then alphabetical order—she was not fully prepared to engage. Anything he said during that time was unlikely to be processed. Neither of them were morning people—she thought he knew that.

"My apologies," he said. "I should have known better. But, pumpkin, before you go upstairs to Mrs. Banerjee's, there's something I wanted to talk to you about."

Sutton's brain began to arrange the lines of code. Her dad was going on a fancy date with a woman he had seen seventeen times. He had forgotten their very well-established morning routine, which meant he'd been distracted, and he wanted to have a serious conversation with her.

Forget guiding her robot through a maze in a minute—now Sutton needed to figure out how to turn back time! Back to a time before her dad ever met this Elizabeth Paz. Because dating was one thing, but this sounded like it was leading to a proposal and a ring and a wedding and—

"Your mom called."

The lines of code scattered. "What? Why didn't you let me talk?"

"She was in a hurry."

"So she should have talked to me, not you!"

Sutton was used to her mom being way down at the bottom of the southern hemisphere, but this time it had been almost a month since they'd talked. Between the time difference and questionable satellite phones at the research station in Antarctica where her mom studied emperor penguins, she almost never called.

"The thing is, honey, she needed to talk to me. To make sure I had things covered here." He reached out and squeezed Sutton's hand. "Her return has been delayed."

Sutton snatched her hand back. She felt her ears getting hot and tears pricking at her eyes. Now she wanted to knock the entire bookcase over.

"I'm really, really sorry, pumpkin. The migration patterns are changing, you know, so the penguins are unpredictable and she really has to stay to monitor them . . ."

Sutton knew way more than she wanted to know about the stupid penguins' migration patterns. But the only migration she cared about was her mom's.

"Maybe I should have waited to tell you. Do you want me to stay home tonight?"

Of course she wanted him to stay home! He'd just ambushed her with terrible news, and on top of it, he was heading off on a fancy date that was leading nowhere good. If she showed him how upset she was about her mom, he'd stay home.

But Sutton wasn't a super big fan of showing her feelings.

Also, logic said this course of action would only postpone a proposal. It wouldn't stop it.

Sutton's chest tightened. There were too many feelings to keep hidden. If her dad kept sitting there, staring at her with puppy-dog eyes of concern, she'd burst. "You should go."

It wasn't until after they had trudged upstairs to Mrs. Banerjee's apartment, chased her yappy dog down the hall when the pup made a break for it, and said goodbye that Sutton had the worst realization of all: Her mom was going to miss her tenth birthday.

CHAPTER TWO

Luis

Luis's head was going to explode.

Not in an angry way. In a throat-swelling, chest-bursting, racing-to-the-emergency-room kind of way. He had been so careful—he was *always* so careful—to eat only the food his mom had packed for his overnight at Sawyer's house. And yet here he was, hurtling toward Seattle Children's Hospital. Again.

Every day, Luis lived with Mad-Eye Moody levels of constant vigilance around everything he put in his mouth. His food allergies were sensitive enough that he even had to care what other people were eating, hence the stupid allergy table in his school's lunchroom. (There was no reason he needed to sit at a special table. He knew how to handle an allergen exposure. But stupid school policies are stupid school policies.)

And now he was expected to analyze the diets of people's pets, too?!

Sawyer's pet guinea pig had been so cute, with its quivering little whiskers and tiny pink nose. Luis had been happy and excited to be on a sleepover—his first—but also a little anxious. Then he'd seen the guinea pig. What better way to calm his nerves than to cuddle a bundle of fluff?

When Luis asked if he could hold it, Sawyer had shrugged. "Piglet?" he said. "Sure, if you want."

And when Luis picked Piglet up and nuzzled him against his cheek, he felt better right away. For half a second, anyway. Then he looked closer at the cage and saw something in Piglet's food dish that almost made him drop the wiggly creature. Peanut shells.

Luis was disappointed, sure, but not all that surprised when his throat started swelling up and he broke out in itchy hives. It happened. Kind of a lot, honestly. He didn't have to eat peanuts to have a mild allergic reaction to them. He just had to be near somebody who'd been eating peanuts recently. Even if that somebody was a guinea pig. The littlest bit of peanut dust on Piglet's fur, and Luis's regular-kid sleepover was over.

His mom would have sighed and given him some Benadryl and a lecture about being more careful. But Sawyer's mom was running red lights and breaking traffic laws right and left. Now, that was kind of exciting. A lot more exciting than petting a guinea pig, anyway.

A text alert went off in the front seat, and Mrs. Lawson chucked her phone back at them. It almost hit Sawyer in the head. "See who it is!" she shrieked, taking a corner like a race car driver.

"Really, Mrs. Lawson, I'm fine—"

"Your mom says she's meeting us at the hospital," Sawyer said, reading the text.

Luis groaned.

"What is it, honey? We're almost there!" If possible, Sawyer's mom sped up.

Luis's mom had plans tonight, which was why Luis was sleeping over at Sawyer's. His mom almost never had exciting plans of her own. Sure, lately she'd gone on some dates with a new guy she seemed to like a lot. But tonight wasn't just a hike or a movie. Luis had spent at least an hour helping his mom pick out what she would wear. (His mom thought the dress with the velvet trim was too fancy, but Luis thought a French restaurant and a night at the opera was exactly the time to wear the fanciest thing in one's closet. Especially if one wore a dingy lab coat all day, every day.)

Then she spent another hour going over all of Luis's food allergies with Sawyer's mom before she would leave. Luis had sworn everything would be fine—she should go and have fun.

And now she would miss her fancy night—she would never be able to tell him what escargots tasted like!—because she was on her way to the emergency room. Again.

The wheels screeched as Sawyer's mom skidded to a stop in front of the sliding glass doors at the emergency room. She leapt out of the front seat.

"You can't park here, Mrs. Lawson," Luis said when she yanked his passenger door open. "Only ambulances—"

"Come on, Sawyer," she barked as she pulled Luis from the car.

"Ma'am," said an orderly pushing an empty wheelchair back toward the hospital. "We keep this area clear for the ambulances—"

"This child is on death's door!" she shrieked.

The orderly looked at Luis. Luis waved. "Hi, Jerome."

"Oh hey, kid," he said. "Peanut allergy, right?"

"Everything allergy, more like," Sawyer muttered.

Mrs. Lawson pushed Luis into the empty wheelchair and started to grab it from the orderly.

"Ma'am," Jerome said firmly. "I'll take him inside. Park your car in the lot, please."

"It's really okay," Luis said to Sawyer's mom, his tongue growing thick in his mouth. "I know Jerome."

Mrs. Lawson struggled with her conscience for a moment, but then an approaching siren wailed. "Get back in the car!" she yelped at Sawyer, and finally Luis was rolling through the sliding doors toward the familiar bright lights and antiseptic smell of the hospital.

"Hey, sugar," the woman behind the desk said with a slow smile when she saw Luis coming her way. "What was it this time?"

"A guinea pig," Luis said. Her eyebrows slid up

her forehead. "I didn't eat it! Just petted it! How was I supposed to know it had peanut breath?"

She chuckled and waved at Jerome. "Bring him on through to triage."

Luis was getting settled in the little in-between room where they'd take his blood pressure and heart rate and stuff, when he heard Mrs. Lawson shouting in the waiting room.

"I've got his insurance cards! I've got his identification info! His mother is on her way!"

A young nurse in Star Wars scrubs stepped into the room. "Is that lady with you?" she asked Luis, her accent thick like his abuelo's. She strapped the blood pressure cuff onto Luis's arm as he nodded.

"She thinks I'm going to die."

The nurse watched the numbers on the blood pressure cuff, then released the tight band from his arm. "Probably not today."

By the time Luis's mom arrived, he'd been moved back to a little room where he'd gotten some medicine that was making him dopey. A Mariners game played soundlessly on the television.

"Oh, love!" Her strawberry-blond curls had slipped out of the fancy twist she'd done for her date, and her normally serene blue eyes were wild.

Luis hated that expression on her face; it always lurked right under the surface, waiting to burst through. She had that exact look way back in kindergarten, when Luis had been stung by a bee during recess and gone into anaphylactic shock for the first time. He'd been rushed to the emergency room then, too. He could have died. He almost did.

Horrible expression or not, Luis froze his mom there in the doorway for a second, imagined sketching her, painting her, framing her. He'd always thought she looked like Anne of Green Gables, all grown up. His mother's fair features were so different from Luis's dark ones, inherited from his father, that people sometimes didn't even believe they were related.

He forced himself to stay awake. "I'm fine, Mom. You didn't have to come."

"Of course I had to come!" She kissed his forehead, and her perfume smelled like the lilac tree in their backyard that only bloomed for a few weeks every spring but filled the whole yard with its fragrance while it did. "I wanted you to know I'm here. Now I'm going to track down the doctor."

She swept out of the room, but the lilac smell

lingered. Only for a second, though. It was quickly replaced with the harsh smell of hospital cleaners.

As usual, Luis's allergies were messing things up. Only not just for him—this time for his mom, too.

CHAPTER THREE

Sutton

The robot maze was spread out on Mrs. Banerjee's kitchen table, but there still hadn't been any progress. Sutton had been hoping her upstairs neighbor could help. She was retired now, but she had been a computer science professor a million years ago.

As soon as she'd seen Sutton's face, though, Mrs. B had insisted on making her cure for everything—spices and honey stirred into warm milk, which bloomed a brilliant yellow when she added a spice called turmeric.

"There'll be plenty of time to get that robot through the maze," she said.

And now there would be. More time than she'd expected, anyway, since Sutton's mom's trip had been delayed. Stupid penguins.

Mrs. Banerjee hadn't even finished making Sutton's golden milk before her dad returned from his date. "Knock knock," he said, sticking his head inside way earlier than he should have returned home.

A tiny seed of hope sprouted in Sutton's chest. Maybe things had ended with Elizabeth? But then shame washed over her; she did want her dad to be happy, after all.

The thing was, while her mom was off studying the tuxedoed creatures, Sutton's dad was her very own emperor penguin—the papa bird who stayed and watched the baby while the mama penguin went off to do important things far away. That was how it had always been with emperors, and it was how it had been for Sutton and her dad for almost as long as she could remember.

What would it mean for their little colony if Elizabeth came in and disrupted it all? A papa penguin who wasn't focused on the survival of his chick was sure to lose it on the ice, where it would freeze or be trampled. Alone.

"What are you doing here?" Sutton said at the same time that Mrs. Banerjee hollered, "Don't let Moti out!"

Dad jumped inside and slammed the door as Moti hurtled toward him, throwing herself at his legs. Sutton's tiny robot spun in circles when it was supposed to be moving backward.

"Everything all right?" Mrs. Banerjee asked as Sutton's dad joined her at the kitchen table. "Would you like some golden milk, Martin?"

"Sure, that would be great." He looked at the spinning robot. "Still giving you trouble?"

Sutton scowled, but then Mrs. Banerjee set a steaming yellow cup of goodness in front of her. The creamy golden milk was a miracle cure for the blues, and Sutton didn't even believe in miracles.

"My date was cut short," he said. "Elizabeth's son had an allergic reaction, and she had to rush to the ER."

"Oh dear." Mrs. Banerjee placed a mug of golden milk in front of Sutton's dad and cradled her own in her wrinkly hands. "If you want to join them at the hospital, Sutton is welcome to stay the night."

He sipped his milk. "I don't think it's as serious as all that. Unfortunately, seems like these hospital trips are a pretty regular occurrence for them. Since I'm suddenly free for dinner, I thought maybe my best girl would like to check out the new pho place on the corner."

Nothing quite like being someone's second choice. Especially when that someone was the one parent who had always been there before.

"I'm not hungry." Sutton plucked the tiny robot off the maze and powered it down. Maybe it needed charging. Maybe *she* needed charging. But a good night of sleep wasn't going to change the fact that her dad would have rather had dinner with Elizabeth tonight.

And worse, her mom wouldn't be home for her birthday.

She tucked the bot carefully into its carrying pod and began to fold up the maze.

"Sutton, I know you're upset about your mom—"

She stood quickly and knocked the edge of the table, splashing golden milk everywhere. "Oh, Mrs. B, I'm sorry!"

Mrs. Banerjee made soft shushing noises as she gathered some rags and began to wipe up the mess.

"Milk spills," she said, like it was the most obvious fact. The Earth orbits the sun. Moti barks at anything that moves. Your parents have more important things to think about than you, Sutton.

"Mom is so sorry about the delay." Dad guided Sutton back down into her chair. "They're so close to completing this study. It's a really important piece of securing the funding—"

"But it's my birthday!" Sutton cried.

Mrs. Banerjee sat down on her other side and took Sutton's hand. "Your mama loves you so much."

Yeah, Sutton's mom loved her. She knew that. But it was always going to be more important to keep tracking where the penguins waddled than come home to be with her daughter. And the worst thing was, Sutton knew the penguins were in trouble. Melting ice and limited food supplies meant lots of penguins were dying. And the ones that survived were trying to find new breeding grounds to hatch and raise their chicks, places with more food and better conditions.

The penguins were kind of like her robot—trying to do what they were programmed to do, except something had gone wrong. Animal instincts were different from computer code, though. They could adapt to changes in their environment. They had to, in order to survive. And the scientists were doing what they could to help.

If her mom was going to keep focused on her work, then Sutton would too. That was what scientists did. They stuck with the experiment and kept trying until they made their breakthrough, no matter what. At least the great ones, like Mom. Like Sutton would be someday. She would accept the extra time as a gift and make sure she got her bot through the maze by the time her mom got home.

When she finally arrived, Mom would see the results of Sutton's dedication and know that the whole time she'd been tracking penguins, Sutton had been doing her own serious work. Sure, they weren't together, working on their projects, but if Sutton squinted at it sideways, it was like they were.

Kind of.

But she wasn't going to make any progress here. Mrs. Banerjee and Dad were too caught up in all the feelings. And feelings were useless. Sutton needed to think like a scientist right now. Moti appeared at Sutton's feet, nudging her shin.

"I have to take Moti out," Sutton said.

"Well . . . okay, honey," her dad said. "Maybe Moti could walk with us to the pho place and we could order takeout? Could we bring you something, Mrs. B?"

"I need to be alone." Sutton abandoned her robot and headed for the little rack by the door where Moti's leash hung. "May I borrow Moti, Mrs. B?"

"Of course."

"Sutton—"

"We'll talk later, Dad," she said, wrestling a very wiggly Moti into her harness. "I need to brainstorm."

He'd understand that. Sometimes they'd be in the middle of dinner and he'd leap up and dive for his cello, consumed by a need to work out some little composition in his head. He wouldn't argue with commitment to one's work.

"All right," he finally said. "If you're sure you're okay."

Sutton wasn't okay—yet. But she would be.

CHAPTER FOUR

Luis

Luis was never going to touch a guinea pig again.

Or any animal with the peanut munchies. It wasn't worth it. It wasn't worth the stress he'd caused Mrs. Lawson. Sawyer probably wouldn't ever want him to come over again. It wasn't worth the headache from the medicine they'd given him in the ER. It wasn't worth the look on his mom's face when she burst into the emergency room, half expecting him to be dead. And it definitely wasn't worth the massive bill that would come from the hospital in a few weeks.

To be on the safe side, he should probably never leave the house again.

"Let me get into some pj's," his mom said as they walked in the front door. "And then we'll snuggle up and read, okay? We left off on such an exciting part!"

"I don't feel like reading." Luis went straight to his bedroom and collapsed onto his bed.

"Sweetheart?" His mom hovered above him. "What's wrong?" She held a cool hand to his forehead. Luis not wanting to read was an even more alarming symptom than when his head swelled up like a puffer fish.

"I'm just tired," he said, which wasn't even a lie. "You can go change."

He was tired. Tired of messing things up. Tired of missing out. Tired of reading about adventures he would never have because so many things in the outside world could kill him. Or at least make him super itchy.

He was still sprawled on his bed, glaring at his ceiling, when his mom came in a few minutes later, wearing her raggedy old UW sweatshirt and the brightly woven pajama bottoms she got on their last trip to Guatemala.

"I'm making hot cocoa," she said. "You sure you don't want to read?"

"Why?" he grumbled, kicking a stuffed narwhal off his bed. Good thing it wasn't a real narwhal—he was probably allergic. "So I can read about all the things I can't actually do?"

"Oh, Luis." His mom picked the narwhal up off the floor and stroked it like she wanted to stroke him but was afraid he would kick her if she did. "I know this was a disappointment. But there will be more sleepovers, I promise."

Luis looked at his mom skeptically. She would let him try another sleepover?

She gave a sheepish smile. "In a couple of years, maybe. But you do lots of interesting things! I mean, you're writing a book! How many ten-year-olds are writing a book?!"

He curled up and faced the wall. "I'm still groggy from the medicine." Which was also not a lie. But mostly, he didn't want to talk about this anymore.

After she tucked him in and left the room, though, Luis couldn't sleep. For one thing, it wasn't even dark outside yet. But also, now he couldn't stop thinking about his book. His mom acted so proud of him, but why? He had scribbled in a notebook. He hadn't let her read what he'd written so far, so she didn't even know if it was any good. It probably wasn't.

From his bed, he could just reach the notebook on the corner of his desk. He'd spent a long time in the bookstore, picking out the perfect one. Some of them had really cool designs, like rockets or dragons or volcanoes. But he wanted to tell his very own story, and he didn't want the cover of the notebook to influence what he wrote. So he'd picked one in a soft brown, with little curlicues engraved up and down the edges. It looked like the kind of book you might pick up in an old, dusty library, and there would be no way to tell what kind of story it held until you started reading.

Luis opened the cover and looked at the first lines he had written almost a year ago: *Penelope Bell didn't look like a hero, with her knobby knees, frizzy hair, and too-thick glasses. And she wasn't yet. But she would be.*

Luis had been inventing characters with his mom since he was in preschool. First it had been a mouse who lived in the cupboard above the refrigerator, where neither of them could ever reach.

(This was, no doubt, heavily influenced by *The Mouse and the Motorcycle*.)

Then there'd been a fairy-sprite character called Barnabus Twixley, who they used to blame when something went wrong. *Oh, silly Barnabus forgot to pick up his wet towels!* Or, *That Barnabus! He knows he's not supposed to put the rice milk container back in the fridge empty!*

But Penelope Bell was the first character who was all Luis's own. She was the first character who faced real dangers, but went out and did things anyway. Important things. At first he only daydreamed about her, and then he started making little sketches, and finally he'd started writing bits of her story down.

Like all good fantasy characters, Penelope Bell's life had been miserable before she'd been invited to the Whitlow School for Extraordinary Children. Her parents were both dead (obviously), her guardian great-aunt treated her like a servant, and her only education came from a dusty set of books in her great-aunt's attic.

But then one day, while weeding her great-aunt's vegetable patch, she'd been stung by a bee. Not just any bee. This bee had been sent by an evil force to make Penelope into a foot soldier in his drone army. Deprived of love, she was supposed to be easy to mold into a heartless force of darkness. What the evil force didn't realize was Penelope had too much good in her heart for the evil to take root, and instead the sting awakened powers she never knew she'd had.

And those powers got her a full scholarship to the Whitlow School, which was filled with misfit kids like her, all sleeping and eating and living together in dorms, away from the guardians who would hold them back if they understood their full potential.

It felt so great to write, at first. When Luis's mom wouldn't let him go to last year's end-of-school party at Golden Gardens because there were likely to be bees buzzing around the picnic food, Penelope stood up to her great-aunt and gave a stirring monologue on how she wouldn't be held back any longer. When he had to stare longingly at the rest of the cafeteria while sitting at the allergy table with two kindergartners, a second grader, and a sixth grader who always had earbuds in, Penelope became prefect and captain of the flyster team (a complicated sport involving fireballs, tightrope walking, and trained falcons).

Penelope could even pet a guinea pig, if she wanted to, though she probably wouldn't. She was more into birds of prey.

But now Penelope made Luis mad. Sitting around writing words on a page was not anything like throwing a fireball to win a flyster match. How had writing ever made him feel better?

It was fine to pretend that a girl like Penelope, with nothing going for her, could somehow out of nowhere be magically anointed by the bee sting that would change her life.

But all Luis's bee sting had gotten him was a mom obsessed with keeping him safe from the world.

CHAPTER FIVE

Sutton

Moti tugged on the leash with a lot more force than seemed reasonable for her size. But Sutton was prepared—she and Moti were regular brainstorming buddies. She looped the strap around her hand as she pushed out of the apartment building and onto the sidewalk. Moti immediately lunged for a passing pit bull.

"Hello, there," said a tiny and extremely wrinkly old woman with wispy hair sticking out all over like a mad scientist's. She was basically the human version of Moti, except a lot slower. While the pit bull, Frank, wasn't officially a guide dog, Sutton was pretty sure he did most of the seeing for the two of them.

"Hello, Mrs. Leroy."

Frank stood patiently while Moti charged in and around his legs.

"Hello, Simpson." Mrs. Leroy called Sutton a different name every time she saw her. It was always a name that was commonly a last name, and Sutton figured that was close enough. Names mattered, of course, but once a person got to be as old as Mrs. Leroy, their brain was probably full of too many names to keep straight.

"Hey, Sutton!"

She looked up to see Sabina and Sadiq, the twins who lived on the fifth floor, hurrying from the building to their mom's waiting minivan. From the looks of their uniforms, they were off to soccer. It was always something sporty with them.

She waved.

Mrs. Leroy had been fishing around in her bag and now emerged with an enormous dog treat, which she held out for Moti. But she couldn't bend over, and Moti couldn't reach it, no matter how much she jumped. Besides which, the treat was bigger than Moti's head.

"I'll give that to her," Sutton said. "Thank you, Mrs. Leroy."

Frank led Mrs. Leroy away, and Sutton broke a small piece off the end of the treat for Moti.

She watched Sabina and Sadiq's minivan pull away from the curb. It was covered in stickers for the various teams the Khan twins played on. Sutton had gone to watch them in a volleyball tournament last month, sitting between their mom and dad, eating popcorn and cheering when they cheered. She liked the twins' dedication to the sport. She did not like the gymnasium full of shouting people. And the whole time, she hadn't been able to shake the memory that her mother hadn't been there at the All-State Science Fair last year.

If Dad was getting serious with Elizabeth, maybe he would be too busy to go to this year's science fair. Then she'd have no one.

Moti dragged Sutton to the crosswalk, and they headed toward the community pea patch across the street from the apartment building. Sutton preferred to tend her plants indoors, but the pea patch was pretty neat for the other apartment dwellers in the area who wanted a little plot of land to call their own.

Sutton waved at Zadie, the college student who could almost always be found sitting on her bit of earth with a textbook. Right now, though, she was on a gardening break, weeding.

Moti zoomed along the paths between the plots, and Sutton let her retractable leash unspool all the way. A siren wailed and Moti stopped suddenly, her head whipping around to track the sound. But then it faded out, and she was off again.

Moti had been born into a litter of puppies. But she hadn't seen her mom or littermates since Mrs. B brought her home from the shelter five years earlier. Did Moti remember them? If she saw them on the street, would she recognize them as her family?

Probably not. But a human child who'd been separated from her parents as a baby probably wouldn't recognize them years later either.

Sutton hadn't been a baby when her parents divorced. She'd been five. And she still got to see her mom, at least sometimes. She barely remembered when they all lived together. Their life as it was now was normal. She was used to it. If her dad married someone else, though, who knew what could change? Maybe they'd have to move again. Maybe they wouldn't want Sutton to live with them.

There was too much uncertainty in the whole situation. Sutton wanted to be able to write a code with a predictable outcome for how things were supposed to go. At the very least, she should be able to write the code to make a mini-bot go through a maze.

If she couldn't do that, she wouldn't even have a shot at All-State Science Fair. Honestly, she was getting behind if she wanted to be a great kid coder. Sutton's dad had shown her a magazine article about "top teenage coders," but there was one kid featured who was eleven. The magazine article only featured boys, though, and Sutton had pinned it to the wall above her bed for motivation. She was going to be featured in an article like that one day. Maybe one day soon.

It was an ambitious goal. But Sutton was an ambitious girl.

Moti had reached the end of the retractable leash and was still tugging ferociously.

"What are you hunting?" Sutton called after her. They often strolled through the pea patch in the evening, especially now during the Seattle summer, when it stayed light until nearly ten o'clock. They'd say hello to the regulars who tended their little bits of green in the middle of the city, and sometimes they'd sit on a bench near the drinking fountain to bark at squirrels. (Moti, not Sutton.)

But this time Moti was on a mission. The little furball was so motivated, in fact, that she tugged hard enough to pop the leash out of Sutton's hand, and it went clattering down the path as Moti ran, unrestrained.

"Moti!" Sutton ran too. They were safe in the community garden, but it wasn't all that big. If Moti reached the busy downtown street and kept running, something terrible could happen! There wouldn't be enough golden milk in the world to fix that.

Sutton reached the sidewalk on the other side of the garden. A city bus zoomed past, and she stumbled back a few steps. A dog barked, but it was howlier than Moti's bark, and Sutton couldn't see where the howl-bark had come from, anyway. Where was that little rascal?

"Over here, Sutton!"

She whipped around toward the pea patch and saw Mr. Wong waving his cane at her.

"Moti's here with me!"

Sutton took a second to breathe, hunching over and wrangling her heart back to its normal rate. It still pounded even though Moti was all right. That was biology—her brain had sent the signal to the body that there was danger! Fight or flight! Even the sight of Moti safe and sound was not enough to turn off her body's warning system so easily.

But Sutton could admire the way the human body worked another time. She hurried over to Mr. Wong's carefully tended plot of vegetables. He chuckled and pointed with his cane to the far corner, where Moti lay curled up with Mr. Wong's cat, Freckles, nuzzling him like they hadn't seen each other in years.

Mr. Wong lived next door to Mrs. Banerjee. At first, Mrs. Banerjee and Mr. Wong had tried to keep their animals apart. Cats and dogs, after all. They feared a flufftastrophe. But Moti and Freckles were undaunted. Freckles would hop from his balcony over to Mrs. Banerjee's and slip in whenever she opened the sliding door to water her plants. Or Moti would bolt out Mrs. Banerjee's front door and run down the hall to claw at Mr. Wong's door as Freckles yowled from inside.

Finally their owners gave in, and the two animals were instant soul mates.

Moti begged for walks whenever Mr. Wong and

Freckles were out working in their garden. Maybe she had an uncanny sense that her feline friend had left the building. Or maybe she simply heard Mr. Wong's cane tapping down the hallway and made a good guess where they were heading.

If Mr. Wong ever moved to another building, Sutton would miss him a lot. For one thing, Mr. Wong always gave her money in a red envelope on Chinese New Year. And he never pestered her with questions when she came and sat near his pea patch plot with her tablet. Her dad would miss him too— Mr. Wong watched baseball with him and brought them fresh dumplings whenever he made a batch. But Moti would be the saddest of all if Freckles ever moved.

Or maybe not. Maybe Moti wouldn't sit around being sad. Maybe Moti would use her animal instincts to find her best friend, no matter where he had gone, like she had found Freckles and Mr. Wong in the pea patch when Sutton hadn't even noticed they were there.

Penguins had the same instincts, traveling up to seventy-five miles to their breeding ground, through a white, barren land covered in snow. And then returning on the same route back to the sea. It had to be a rude surprise to realize those routes that had always worked before didn't work anymore. But the penguins were adapting, trying to find new breeding grounds, and going against the instincts they'd always followed.

If the penguins could chart a new course, then surely Sutton could get her bot through a maze. Right now she needed to know something was going to turn out the way she expected it to.

---- ----> CHAPTER SIX

Luis

The next morning, Luis banged around the kitchen, not even trying to keep it down, even though the soothing tones of his mom's yoga video drifted from the other room. Yoga time was sacred time. He was supposed to honor that.

Instead, he made as much noise as possible.

He didn't know exactly what he was mad about. His mom hadn't done anything wrong. The stupid guinea pig hadn't even done anything wrong.

But everything was somehow wrong, anyway.

"Love?" his mom finally said, appearing in

the doorway with a less blissed-out look than she usually had post-yoga. "Can I help you find something?"

Luis slammed another cupboard door and then sank into a kitchen chair. "Sorry, Mom. Nothing sounds good."

She sat down across from him. "Kinda in a funk, huh?"

He scowled at the table.

"What if I make some French toast? And then we call your abuelos?"

Luis brightened. His mom had a way of working magic with gluten-free bread, egg substitute, and rice milk to make the best French toast ever. But talking to his dad's parents in Guatemala would be even better than an excellent breakfast. Luis got to see his mom's parents all the time—they only lived across the bridge in Issaquah. But a video call with his abuelos was a special treat.

Once he'd had his fill of sticky goodness, they set up the laptop and made the call. It rang three times before his abuelo's face filled the screen.

"¡Luisito! ¡Mi nieto favorito!"

Luis was his grandparents' only grandson, but it was still nice to be their favorite.

"Hola, don Miguel," Luis's mom said to her father-in-law. "¿Qué tal?"

"Bien, bien, canche. Y ustedes, ¿todo bien?" Without waiting for an answer, Luis's abuelo called over his shoulder for his wife. "¡Alma!"

Soon she was there too, the lines of her face multiplying as she smiled at the sight of Luis on her grainy screen. "¡Ay, Luis, amorcito! ¿Cómo estás?"

"I'm good, Abuela. How are you?" He could have said that much in Spanish. Her face always lit up when he spoke what he could. But he was shy, knowing how the words would tangle on his tongue.

"Todo bien, gracias a Dios," she said. She continued on, updating him on all of the tíos and tías and cousins he barely knew, speaking a mile a minute in the Spanish that Luis understood but couldn't speak very well.

"¿Cuándo nos vas a visitar?" his abuelo said when his wife finally stopped talking. "You spend summer in your homeland!" He always suggested Luis come spend the summer in Guatemala. Luis never knew what to say. His mom wasn't even comfortable letting him go on field trips, much less travel to another country for an entire summer without her.

If his dad were alive, it would be different. They'd

go all together, like they did once, before Papi got sick. But Luis had been too young then to remember anything now.

"Maybe when Luis is a little older," Mom said. Like always.

"Si pues," Abuelo said.

"Luisito, you write your book still?" Abuela's English wasn't perfect, but it was a lot better than Luis's Spanish.

He shifted in the kitchen chair, which suddenly felt unbearably hard. "Sort of?"

"¿Qué 'sort of'?"

"I guess I'm stuck," he admitted, avoiding his mother's curious gaze. "It seems kinda pointless."

"Ay no," Abuelo said. "Stories are never pointless. You just need some inspiración. You need to go somewhere or do something que te despierta. What about ese museo you took me to when I visited? The one with the walls like ocean waves?"

Luis's abuelos had visited Seattle for the first time a couple of years earlier. They'd done all the tourist stuff—Pike Place Market, the Space Needle, a ferry out to the islands. Luis had also taken them to some of his personal favorite places—the Central Library downtown with a children's section the size of most branch libraries; the Fremont troll, a giant statue under a bridge; and the Museum of Pop Culture, better known as the MoPOP.

The MoPOP was the least boring museum ever. Before you even got inside, you could tell it was going to be awesome. The outside of the building was like a sculpture by an artist, with wavy metallic walls, wild colors, and a strange, twisty shape plucked straight out of an alien world.

Inside, it only got better. The exhibits weren't dusty old fossils or paintings by dead white guys. They were about things like Marvel superheroes; rock and roll history; video games; and fantasy and sci-fi books, movies, and TV shows.

"We haven't been to the MoPOP in a while!" his mom said. "Buena idea, don Miguel. Gracias."

They chatted for a few more minutes and made plans to talk again soon. Then his abuelos were gone, off in a faraway country, and all Luis had to remember them by were the Guatemalan handicrafts all around the house—mementos of the years his mom spent with her husband in his homeland before they settled in Seattle.

"What do you think?" his mom said. "How about a trip to the MoPOP?"

Luis nodded. Inspiration was striking already, even before he'd gone to the museum. What if the MoPOP could not only boost his spirits, but also make up for the date his mom had missed?

"Yeah, and could we invite someone?"

"Sure, honey." She started to clear the dishes off the table. "Who'd you have in mind?"

"Well, the man you've been seeing . . . he has a daughter, right?"

CHAPTER SEVEN

Sutton

The bot was finally turning right!

Sutton had woken up way earlier than usual, with a sudden realization that maybe the problem wasn't the software, but the hardware. She had spread out the maze on the kitchen table before she even started watering her plants. She was filled with hope and possibility. She could get the bot through the maze! Yesterday had been a frustrating blip, but it was all going to turn out all right!

Of course, after she made an adjustment that got the bot to turn right, it only went halfway down the passage before it turned and doubled back again.

"No!" Sutton wailed. "Keep going! No one told you to turn around!"

"Hey, sweetheart." Her dad appeared in the doorway, running a hand through rumpled hair. "You're up early."

"Not prepared to engage," Sutton muttered, squeezing the buttons on the side of the bot to recalibrate it.

"To be fair, you're engaging with the bot," he pointed out, taking a seat at the kitchen table. "So you could maybe spare a few words for your dear old dad."

"It's still not working," Sutton grumbled.

"Maybe it needs a break."

"It's fully charged."

"Maybe *you* need a break."

Something in his voice distracted Sutton from the problems of her bot. She looked up.

"We've been invited to the MoPOP."

"The what?"

"You know, the Museum of Pop Culture? It's by the Space Needle. That funky building with the colorful walls?"

Sutton could picture the building, even though

she usually averted her eyes when they passed it. It gave her a headache. "Who invited us?" Her dad was forever trying to set her up on playdates. Sutton was too old for playdates, but he never believed her when she said she had all the friends she wanted. Sure, her robotics team had quit meeting for the summer. Sabina and Sadiq were always off doing something sportsy. And Luna on the sixth floor had left to spend the summer with her grandparents.

But not everybody wanted a million friends.

"Actually . . ." He picked up the bot and started fidgeting with it. Sutton snatched it back. "You know this woman I've been dating for a while? Elizabeth?"

Sutton froze. She didn't actually know Elizabeth. They hadn't met. Not that she wanted to meet Elizabeth.

"Elizabeth's son Luis is right around your age."

"The one with the guinea pig."

"Right, yes. I mean, he doesn't have a . . . never mind. They have a membership at the museum. And they're going today. We thought it might be a nice chance for you and Luis to get to know each other!"

It was nothing against Luis, but Sutton didn't really want to get to know him. The idea of meeting his mom was bad enough. Once the kids got introduced, it was all downhill to the wedding!

Sutton's life wasn't perfect as it was, but the variables were manageable. She knew what to expect. If her dad got married, what then? To start: Where would they all live? The apartment wasn't big enough for four. And Sutton didn't want to live on cutesy Queen Anne Hill, where Luis and his mom lived. She was a city girl!

Sutton and her dad had their South Lake Union life perfectly mapped out—they had their farmers' market and their pea patch and Mrs. B. and their library. Sutton had morning oatmeal and the periodic table of elements and Moti.

Maybe Elizabeth wouldn't approve of home-schooling, and Sutton would have to go to Luis's school! She would have to stop eating whatever Luis was allergic to! There were too many variables to consider.

"It's not a big deal," her dad said in a rush. "Just hanging out, no pressure. It would give your brain a chance to focus on something else, and I'll bet you'll come back knowing exactly what this little guy needs!"

Her dad reached for the bot again, and Sutton cupped her hand over it.

"I don't know. My stomach doesn't feel too great."

"Probably because you haven't had breakfast yet."

Drat. "I'm supposed to walk Moti this morning."

"Already called Mr. Wong. He's going to cover for you."

Double drat. "I was going to see if Sabina and Sadiq wanted to . . . shoot hoops."

He looked at her skeptically, seeing that for the bald-faced lie it was. "Pretty sure they're in Yakima for a tournament this weekend."

Sutton sighed. Her dad was clearly not giving up. At least at a museum, they could focus on the exhibits and not have to talk to each other. "Fine."

"Great!" He jumped up. "Then get some breakfast, get dressed, and we'll hit the road. We're going to swing by Queen Anne and pick them up."

"That's out of our way." Sutton and her dad could walk to the MoPOP.

"Queen Anne isn't far. Elizabeth's car is on the fritz. Let's leave in twenty, okay?"

It was an alarmingly quick drive to the top of Queen Anne Hill, a beautiful neighborhood of charming old homes, some tiny and some enormous. Sutton had always thought Queen Anne homes looked like colorful confections in the window of a fancy pastry shop, all with their own yards and so different from Sutton's shiny downtown apartment building across from a community garden.

Now the neighborhood seemed kind of sickly sweet.

But as they drove along Queen Anne Avenue, Sutton had to admit it was sort of nice, like a small town in the middle of a big city, with cute little shops and people stopping to chat as they walked their dogs.

Sutton had that in South Lake Union, too. People sold things and walked dogs and talked to one another everywhere. Queen Anne Hill wasn't special.

Her dad pulled up in front of a house that was more artisan cupcake than giant wedding cake. The front yard had that weird no-plant landscaping that was mostly wood chips and whimsical garden sculptures, and the little house was a cheery bright blue, with a tidy front porch and solar panels on top.

Her dad climbed out of the car. Sutton didn't move.

"Hon?" He poked his head back in. "I promise Luis doesn't bite."

"Have you met him?"

"I . . . have not."

"More than forty thousand people go to the emergency room every year due to bites from another human."

Sutton had learned this while working on a project about the breeds of dog most likely to bite versus the breeds of dogs most likely to do damage when they bite. Since then, she had been extra wary around humans she didn't know. Even some of the ones she did know. Her dad shut the driver's-side door with a sigh. Sutton thought—briefly—she was off the hook. But then he came around the car, opened her door, and crouched on the curb outside. "Hon, I know you're nervous. I know this is weird. We've never done this before. But Elizabeth is special to me. Will you make an effort?"

CHAPTER EIGHT

Luis

Luis sat at the kitchen table, tracing his finger along the quetzal on his mug of hot chocolate. The green bird with an enormous tail was the symbol of Guatemala, the tiny Central American country south of Mexico where his grandparents lived. Where his father had come from.

His dad had come to the United States without speaking much English, leaving behind his family and the world he had known for the first sixteen years of his life. He had flown into Los Angeles and gone to live with a great-aunt he'd never met, all so he could finish high school in the United States and stay for college. The plan had been that he'd return to run the family's restaurant chain after he got his American education, but then he'd met Luis's mom in college, and he stayed.

Talk about an adventure! Even Penelope Bell going off to a boarding school for kids with special powers had nothing on Luis's dad. Luis tried to imagine picking up and moving to a whole other country where he didn't know anyone and didn't speak the language. And the language wasn't the only difference. The food, the customs, the way people interacted with one another . . . his mom had talked enough about her visits to Guatemala that he knew it was really different.

If his dad could do something so amazing, Luis could at least figure out what was next in his story.

He jumped at the sound of a knock at the door. It wasn't a great start to being brave like his dad.

"Oh shoot, I'm in the bathroom!" his mom called. "Can you get it?"

Luis tapped the quetzal on his mug one last time for luck and went to the front door. He opened it to find a tall man in jeans and a Hufflepuff T-shirt.

"Luis?" the man said. "I'm Martin."

The man held his hand out for a handshake. Sometimes when adults did that to a kid, it felt condescending. But with Martin, it felt natural, like he was truly glad to meet him.

"You're a Puff?" Luis said, nodding at Martin's T-shirt. "So am I."

"Excellent. Sutton here's a Ravenclaw." The man looked to his right and found nothing but the potted rosemary on the front porch. He stepped aside to reveal his daughter behind him.

"'Wit beyond measure is man's greatest treasure,'" Luis said, reciting the Ravenclaw motto. The girl looked back at him blankly.

"I'm the real Harry Potter fan in the family," the man explained.

"Martin! Hello!" Luis's mom had emerged from the bathroom, and the girl shrank back behind her dad again. But he stepped inside and she was exposed, out on the doorstep. "And you must be Sutton! It's so nice to meet you!"

The car ride was awkward.

In the front, Martin talked to Luis's mom about her car trouble and the limits of Seattle's public transportation system.

"I like taking the bus," Luis said. "But if it snows, we get stuck."

Sutton looked at Luis like he was speaking another language. But at least she looked at him.

"Because of the hill," he added. "It's so steep, the buses can't get down."

Sutton was quiet. But then a minute later, when Luis was sure she hadn't even been listening, she said, "Soon you won't need to leave the hill anyway. Drones can bring you whatever you need."

At first, Luis thought this was an invitation to conversation. Drones! He could talk about drones! He didn't know anything about them, but that wouldn't stop him from imagining the possibilities.

But then Sutton reached into the seat-back pocket in front of her and pulled out a tablet. She angled it away from him and swiped in silence the rest of the way to the MoPOP.

The first time Luis had visited Seattle's MoPOP, it had been on a school field trip. The visit had been cut tragically short when Kyle McClaren pulled out a sandwich at lunch and sprayed peanut butter crumbs all over Luis while reenacting his favorite episode of *Star Trek*.

That time, Luis wasn't rushed to the emergency

room, because his mom was there as a chaperone, so she knew to dose him with Benadryl. But the medicine made him so sleepy, he had to go home anyway. He'd never gotten to see the *Infinite Worlds of Science Fiction* exhibit.

(Also, it had led to Kyle McClaren and his crew calling Luis "Pokey" ever since, because of the needle he carried around in case he ever needed emergency medicine for an allergic reaction. That led to "Pokey Little Puppy," which was from some old picture book and didn't even make sense as an insult, but they all thought it was hilarious.)

Luis's mom brought him back to the museum, just the two of them, and he loved it so much, they got a membership. The MoPOP was one of the few places where he felt like he could travel to other worlds, even if his mom was always standing by with an EpiPen.

He had been excited to share it with Sutton and her dad. After the mostly silent car ride, he was less excited. But maybe she hadn't been quite ready to meet them. He could understand that—he was excited, but also nervous. This was pretty weird, after all.

When his mom first told Luis she was seeing

someone, as in *seeing*-seeing him—not just a work colleague or a buddy from college, but a man she had been out with several times and wanted to keep seeing—Luis hadn't known what to think.

Part of him wanted to keep his mom all to himself. It had been working pretty well for them so far. But he had noticed a certain look in his mom's eyes when they'd pass a happy couple holding hands on the street, and part of him wondered what it would be like to have a bigger family—two parents, maybe even a sibling or two?

He didn't hate the idea.

"So this is the MoPOP!" Martin said in a cheery voice.

"Have you never been here?" Luis asked.

Martin grinned sheepishly. "I have, actually. Back when it was called the Experience Music Project. But it's been a while!" He clapped his daughter on the shoulder and she winced.

"Sutton," Luis's mom said, "we've spent a lot of time here, so if there's something you'd especially like to see, we're up for whatever."

Sutton shrugged.

"Some of our favorite exhibits are the science fiction and fantasy exhibits. I know you like science."

Sutton nodded.

There was an awkward silence before Martin interjected, "Sutton's really into robotics right now."

"There are lots of robots in the sci-fi exhibits," Luis offered.

Sutton brightened. "Real robots?"

"Well . . . yeah! Like R2D2 and BB-8!" She looked as blank as when he'd recited the Ravenclaw motto. "From *Star Wars*?"

Her face fell. "Oh."

That wasn't the reaction Luis had hoped for. The museum had the best collection of memorabilia from classic sci-fi and fantasy movies anywhere. But maybe she wasn't into *Star Wars*. That was okay. There had to be something that would snag her interest.

Or maybe she was shy. Luis could work with that. He was used to feeling like the weird kid, and he had a strategy when he felt uncomfortable in a new situation: He would try to find someone else who looked even more out of place, and then make it his mission to make *them* feel more comfortable.

"So what kind of robots are your favorites?" he asked, as they headed toward the stairs that led up to the main exhibits.

"Right now I'm working with a mini-bot that has optical and proximity sensors," she said. "And my robotics team is trying to get our robot to apply a Kalman filter."

"Cool," Luis said, even though he had no idea what that meant. "But, like, what's your favorite robot character? From books or movies? They don't only have *Star Wars* stuff here, if that's not your favorite!"

"I've never seen *Star Wars*."

Luis thought Sutton said she'd never seen *Star Wars*, but they were passing the *Nirvana* exhibit at the time, and loud, screaming music streamed into the hallway. Surely he'd misheard. But still, he didn't want to call it out and make her feel weird if she truly had somehow gotten through life without seeing *Star Wars*.

"I love WALL-E," Luis offered. "From the Pixar movie? Have you seen that?"

She shook her head again. She was going to get a headache from all the head shaking. But Luis was determined to break through. He had a mission now. He should ask her questions about herself. People always liked to talk about themselves.

"Tell me about your robot," he said.

She brightened. "Oh! Well our team bot has an ARM9 processor with a Linux-based operating system and four input ports for data acquisition of up to one thousand samples per second."

Luis paused, searching for a response. "Does it have a name?"

"Does what have a name?"

"The robot."

She looked confused for a second.

"I mean, all the great robots have names!" They had finally reached the Science Fiction and Fantasy Hall of Fame, and Luis spread his arms out at all the great robot characters before them.

"They're characters in stories," Sutton said.

"Right, so they have names."

They'd reached an impasse. This was like when his abuelos used a Spanish phrase so local to their region that he couldn't understand it or even figure out its meaning by looking it up.

"Sutton!" her dad called. "Come here!" He motioned her over to see something on the opposite side of the room.

"How's it going?" Luis's mom asked, putting an arm around his shoulder. "Feeling any better? Getting any inspiration?"

Actually, he'd been so distracted by trying to draw Sutton out that he hadn't been dwelling on his story. "Sutton's really quiet," he said.

His mom nodded. "She spends a lot of time alone."

Luis spent a lot of time alone too. But that meant that when he got to hang out with a kid his age, he had a ton to say.

"And her mom is still alive," his mom went on. "So that might make this weirder for her."

Why would that make things weird? She was lucky her mom was still alive. Luis would give anything for his dad to be here. Of course, if his dad were here, his parents would still be married and his mom never would have started dating Martin.

"She's never seen *Star Wars*," he finally said.

His mom grinned. "Maybe we should suggest a movie night!"

CHAPTER NINE

Sutton

Sutton was trying. But she felt like her mini-bot, desperately attempting to get out of the maze with all the wrong lines of code.

No matter what Luis asked her, she didn't have the right answer. Normally she didn't care whether she knew all the references to books and movies and music that other kids knew. If she cared, she could learn those things. But this whole situation was weird. It felt like a job interview.

And if she thought it had been going poorly, she was completely unprepared for Luis's next question.

"Where does your mom live?" he asked as she stared in mild disgust at Luke Skywalker's severed hand from *The Empire Strikes Back*. Not a real severed hand. It was a prop from the movie. But it looked way too real.

Sutton tore her eyes from the gruesome thing and looked at Luis. "Here," she said. "She lives here in Seattle. She has an apartment in our building."

She already felt like a freak. She didn't want to explain how her mom's apartment was empty most of the year, how her mom's true home was with the penguins in Antarctica, and that her mom wouldn't even be home for her tenth birthday. How thinking about her mom made her ache with longing at the same time that it made her fiery mad.

"Hey, guys," her dad said, appearing and placing a hand on Sutton's shoulder. "Should we check out the *Infinite Worlds of Science Fiction* exhibit?"

How many science fiction exhibits did this place have? Sutton was into science—real science. That didn't mean she was into made-up science. That would be like assuming a doctor would love playing Operation. Or like Sutton's mom would enjoy playing with stuffed penguins.

(Sutton had a million stuffed penguins. Other

people gave them to her, never her mom. On her last birthday, Sutton's mom had given her a college-level marine biology textbook and an official McMurdo Station parka, not that it ever got cold enough in Seattle to wear a parka designed for Antarctica.)

But at least following them into yet another exhibit filled with fake-science stuff would get her out of talking to Luis about her mom.

"This is one of my favorite parts of the museum," Elizabeth said, leading them over to the fake cockpit of an imaginary spacecraft. She sat in one of the chairs and motioned for Sutton to join her in the other. "What do you think, Sutton? Shall we join the ranks of Sally Ride and Eileen Collins?"

Sutton sat, begrudgingly impressed Elizabeth knew about Eileen Collins. Everyone knew about Sally Ride, first American woman in space. But not as many people gave credit to Eileen Collins, first female commander of a NASA Space Shuttle. Both were featured in a book of great female scientists her mom had given her, with the inscription, *The next time they write this book, YOU'LL be in it!*

"I love pretending," Elizabeth said. "But I'm not sure I could handle the solitude of space."

The museum cockpit looked nothing like a real

spacecraft's cockpit. But sitting and staring through the window at the painting of a moon on the wall beyond, it suddenly occurred to Sutton that being an astronaut might be kind of cool. Long stretches of time in the quiet vastness of outer space, with only a few other people to interact with. No pressure to socialize or have outside hobbies. Just the work.

"Although," Elizabeth went on, "if you think about it, it's rather like the work your mom does in Antarctica!"

Sutton had never thought of her mom as anything like an astronaut, but it was actually a close comparison. Harsh, dangerous conditions meant only the most dedicated scientists devoted themselves to the work, plus they had limited access to the rest of the world and few other people to interact with.

The difference was, an astronaut couldn't just decide to return home to her family once she was in outer space. A research scientist could arrange a flight home from Antarctica, if it was important enough.

"Come here, Luisito." Elizabeth reached out and tugged Luis onto her lap. "Help me steer this thing to the moon!"

Luis wriggled away. He was probably embarrassed, too old to sit on his mom's lap. He had no idea how lucky he was.

Sutton slipped out of the cockpit chair. "Here," she said. "You can sit here."

She stuck to her dad for the rest of their time in the museum. She knew she was lucky to have him. He wasn't going to ask her anything she didn't want to answer. When Luis or Elizabeth asked one of their endless questions, her dad would pipe up and rescue her. They were a team.

Only, it turned out her teammate didn't see it that way. After they'd dropped Luis and Elizabeth off at their adorable little cupcake of a house, Sutton's dad was ominously quiet all the way home.

When they reached their apartment building, he turned the car off and sat there. "I thought you were going to make an effort," he finally said.

Sutton felt like she'd been punched in the gut. "I did!"

"Did you? Because I saw a lot of shrugging and clamming up and letting me answer questions for you."

"I tried! But I couldn't answer anything right! We didn't have anything in common!"

"Sutton." He ran his hand over his face. "This had

nothing to with whether or not Luis is into robotics or you're into mythological creatures. You find things to talk about with Mrs. B and Mr. Wong. With Sabina and Sadiq. You don't have much in common with any of them. If you were trying to sabotage my relationship with Elizabeth, I hate to disappoint you, but it's not going to work."

Then he got out of the car and headed for the building without even waiting for her.

The tears came instantly. She had tried her best. And there was nothing wrong with Elizabeth or Luis—she liked them fine. But Sutton's worst fears had been confirmed. Her dad's new relationship was pulling him away from her. And soon she'd have nobody.

CHAPTER TEN

Luis

When Luis woke up, sun streamed across his bedroom in big, bold rays. So unlike most June gloom mornings. It had to be a good omen. Weather was always giving warnings of what was to come in Luis's favorite stories. Like, if a story started with a big thunderstorm, you knew it was going to be a spooky one.

Luis used to think this was kind of silly, because the weather did not usually match what was happening in his real life. Happy things could happen on stormy days, and terrible things could happen on perfectly clear ones. But then he started writing his book, and he realized how much weather helped set the mood.

Anyway, books weren't real life. That was the best part about them.

Books were places where Penelope Bell could be swept away from her dreary life to a world of magic and adventure. Where a bee sting didn't mean she had to stay inside for the rest of time, but instead gave her powers to defeat evil. Where she could join forces with other misfit kids—true friends who understood her, even if they were each different in their own way—and change the world.

Once he'd realized he wasn't going to get Sutton to open up no matter how many questions he asked her, Luis had spent the rest of his time at the MoPOP soaking in the inspiration for his story. He'd been too focused on the logic of what might happen next, he'd decided. But it was a fantasy! He needed to let his imagination take over!

Right then the door opened a crack and Luis's mom poked her head in.

"Oh good! You're up!"

Luis's eyes flew to the clock—he was always up before his mom. How was it already almost ten o'clock?!

"All the excitement of the last couple days must have taken it out of you," Mom said, opening the door all the way. She was completely dressed and everything. It was super weird.

And what excitement? There had been no excitement. Just a stupid trip to the emergency room, and the most awkward visit ever to the MoPOP. But when they got home from the museum, Luis had stayed up super late, working on his story with his newly fueled imagination.

All those creators—authors of fantasy novels and actors and filmmakers and cartoonists—they must have felt stuck sometimes. But they had pushed through and made things so great they were now in a museum! They probably stayed up way past their bedtimes all the time when they were young creators. Luis was just following their example. Which could explain why he sort of felt like crawling under the covers and staying there a few more hours.

Then Luis sat bolt upright. "You're missing yoga!" He checked the clock again, in case he'd misread it the first time. But nope, 9:52. Saturday mornings were the only time she got to go to an actual class in a studio. Another thing he'd messed up for his mom.

"That's okay, love," she said, coming in and sitting on his bed. "I wanted to let you rest. I thought maybe we could play some board games, if you feel up to it. Or have a *Harry Potter* movie marathon?"

Luis eyed his notebook on his desk. Mom followed his gaze. "Or do you want to work on your book? You should work on your book!" She jumped up like he needed to give someone CPR and she was standing in the way. "I'll make you a smoothie. Let me know if you need anything!"

Once Mom was bustling around in the kitchen, Luis grabbed his notebook and looked over the pages he'd worked on last night.

Penelope Bell and her friends Stuart and Marjorie had snuck out of their dorm in the middle of the night in order to test the strength of their powers under a full moon. Up until then, teachers had always been monitoring them to make sure they didn't get out of control. But if they were going to defeat the Dark Force, they had to understand their abilities. It had been risky—if a teacher had seen them, they would have been expelled for sure. But sometimes you have to take risks to defeat the Dark Force.

(Luis was still working on the villain's name.

"The Dark Force" sounded too much like "the Dark Lord" mixed with the *Star Wars* "Force," but that's what first drafts were for.)

What he'd written the night before looked good. Messy, but good. So good that his own characters were inspiring him. He didn't want to be limited to living through their experiences. He wanted to get off the page and have his own experiences. He wouldn't sneak out in the middle of the night, of course. But all this inspiration would be pointless if his mom locked him in the house for the rest of his life. Only out in the world would he find what he needed to become a true storyteller.

And he had to start somewhere.

Luis pulled some bills from the little wooden box on his dresser where he kept his money, put on the first clothes he found, and headed out to the kitchen. "I'm going to the corner store," he told his mother as soon as she turned off the blender.

"You're . . . what?"

A quest to the convenience store for new markers wasn't exactly a duel with the darkest forces of evil, but Luis had never done it by himself before. And it was only three blocks to Queen Anne Avenue, the hub of their neighborhood, and its cute little shops, including a convenience store that was sure to have at least a few art supplies.

"My markers are getting dried out," Luis said. "I need some new ones. I'm going to get them."

His mom blinked at him as though he were speaking a different language. "We can go together," she said. "In fact, let's drive to the art supply store. They'll have a much better selection."

"Mom. It's three blocks to the Ave. I'd like to try going by myself." Luis took a deep breath and willed his mom to breathe too. Now she looked like the one who needed a trip the ER. "May I?"

He watched her calculate the odds that he would encounter a bee along the way.

"I'll take my EpiPen," he said. "And some Benadryl. And my phone. I'll only be gone twenty minutes. Then we can have a movie marathon. Please, Mom?"

She came around the counter and took his face between her hands. She leaned their foreheads together. Luis braced for her reasons why he couldn't, why it was too dangerous, why she would need to be the one to run all the errands for the rest of time eternal.

"Oh, love," she said. "You must feel so cooped up. I can't hover over you forever. You go ahead."

Luis scrambled for the door before he could change his mind. "Thank you, Mom!"

She followed him onto their front step. "But text me when you get there!" she called. "And when you're heading back!"

CHAPTER ELEVEN

Sutton

Sutton was not fully prepared to engage. She was even less prepared to engage than usual, after it had taken her forever to fall asleep the night before.

At bedtime her dad had talked to her about the MoPOP. He had this rule about not letting the sun go down on their anger, which meant that if they were cross with each other, they had to hash it out before they went to bed so they could start fresh the next day. But the thing was, if you were angry, you were angry. The rotation of the Earth really had nothing to do with it.

Last night, her dad was the one who'd been angry. Sutton had been more hurt. She'd done her best to explain her side—how she hadn't been trying to sabotage anything, how she'd just been uncomfortable.

She hadn't been fully honest, though. She couldn't tell her dad how worried she was about what would happen to her if Elizabeth took over his heart. That had eaten away at her and she'd lain in bed, staring at the constellation stickers on her ceiling until long after she'd heard her dad talking to Elizabeth on the phone, and bolting the door, and brushing his teeth, and going to bed.

She was out of bed now, but sort of wished she could crawl back in and stay there for the rest of the day. The thing was, that would make her dad want to do more talking, and she was all talked out. She had finished with the succulents and started watering the *Epipremnum aureum* when her dad emerged from his bedroom in jogging clothes.

"I'm going around the lake," he said. "I texted Mrs. Banerjee. She's home if you need anything. And I've got my phone."

Sutton scowled in his general direction. It was too early for human interaction, much less for exercise.

But if he went for his run, there would be one less human to interact with. "Okay," she said.

He kissed the top of her head and peered at her face for a second. "You okay today, pumpkin? We're okay, right?"

"Dad. Not fully prepared to engage," she sighed. "But yeah. We're okay."

He grinned. "Gotcha. We'll talk when I'm back, then. Unless you want to join me on my run? Let the fresh morning air invigorate your senses? Appreciate the beauty of plants that grow in the actual earth?" He danced out of the way as Sutton threatened him with the watering can, and his laughter still echoed even after he'd shut the door behind him.

By the time Sutton was done watering the apartment plants and eating her breakfast, her brain felt less fuzzy. She didn't like to admit it, but all the pretend robots in the MoPOP had inspired her, in their way. Sure, they weren't real. They couldn't actually be programmed to do the things people saw them do in movies.

But they had all been created by people who dreamed up what was possible.

She pulled out a notebook and jotted down a brainstorming list of all the possible things she could try to get her bot through the maze. No idea was too ridiculous! (Even though some definitely were. Singing soothing songs to the bot was not going to work. That had been her dad's idea.)

Her robotics adviser, Ms. Nguyen, always encouraged them to keep an open mind. She also said two minds were better than one. Sutton struggled with this one—she usually preferred to work alone. But Ms. Nguyen had coached three previous teams to the Robotics World Championships, so she had to know what she was talking about.

If Sutton's team wasn't on summer break, it would be a lot easier. She would just bring her bot to a meeting and ask her teammates for ideas. But they were scattered around town, and Ms. Nguyen had left for a summer trip through Europe.

There was one teammate who'd stayed in town. And lived nearby. Sometimes uncomfortably nearby.

Riley Dairman-Bedichek lived on the seventh floor, in fact. She and Sutton had clashed badly when Sutton first joined the robotics team. They'd learned to work together as teammates, mostly, but the truth was they were in constant competition. Even if they wouldn't let the adults see that.

Riley was the best coder Sutton knew, aside from

Ms. Nguyen. If Sutton really wanted to make progress with her bot before her mom got home, she'd have to swallow her pride and ask for help.

Sutton texted her dad so he'd know where she went if he returned early. Then she grabbed the maze, popped the bot into its carrying case, and headed up to the Dairman-Bedicheks' seventh-floor apartment.

Riley's curly-haired mom opened the door before Sutton even had a chance to knock. "Oh, Sutton honey!" she cried. "We were just heading out."

Sutton stepped out of the way and the willowy woman bustled out, followed by her three-year-old, Riley's short-haired mom, and finally, Riley. Her eyebrows shot up. "Hey, Sutton."

"Hey, um." They all kept moving, so Sutton trailed after them to the elevator. "I'm having some trouble with my bot. I thought maybe we could brainstorm?"

Short-Haired Mom held the elevator door, so Sutton got on.

"Oh." Riley looked far too pleased. "I'd be happy to help. But we're going to my grandmother's. I won't be home until tonight."

"Oh."

Curly-Haired Mom squeezed Sutton's shoulders. "I love that you girls are friends! Coding partners! Girl power! Who run the world?!"

"Girls!" sang Short-Haired Mom and the three-year-old, who had obviously seen this routine before.

Riley's cheeks flamed, and she lost all trace of smugness. The elevator doors opened. "Sorry," she mumbled. "Maybe later."

Riley's moms were totally embarrassing. But they were also both there, singing and dancing their way across the lobby. The three-year-old took Riley's hand and dragged her after them. They looked like such a happy family.

Then the elevator doors closed and Sutton was all alone again.

"Come in!" Mrs. Banerjee called over Moti's barks when Sutton knocked a few minutes later. She hadn't been able to bear going back to her empty apartment.

"Mrs. B?" Sutton squeezed inside quickly so Moti couldn't escape. "You shouldn't leave your door unlocked."

"But what if my favorite neighbor drops by and I'm stuck on the couch?"

Moti trailed Sutton as she hurried around the

couch, jumping to get at the treats Sutton always carried. Mrs. Banerjee sat with her legs up, an ice pack on her knee.

"What happened?" Sutton handed Moti a treat to hush her up.

"Oh, well. It turns out if you use your joints for sixty-some years, they start to wear out!"

"Do you need anything? Should I make golden milk? Does Moti need to go out?"

"Mr. Wong just took Moti out, so maybe a little later? For now, I could use your company."

Sutton sank down onto the carpet. At least, she was expecting the carpet. Instead, something hard poked her in the behind. "Ouch!"

"Oh dear, I'm sorry. Why don't you shove those over to the side?"

That's when Sutton noticed a variety of thick white tubes and hard plastic connector thingies scattered across the floor. In the corner, there was a stack of plywood and carpet squares, and a coil of rope.

"What are you making?"

Mrs. B shook her head. "I feel silly now," she said. "The truth is, my knee's acting up because I was kneeling on it, trying to build that thing!"

Some scattered papers on the coffee table caught Sutton's eye. They were plans of some sort. Like building plans. Mrs. B was busy adjusting her ice pack, so Sutton peered at the plans.

"Looks like a jungle gym," she said.

"That's what it is, essentially. A cat condo, I think it's called."

"For Moti?"

"No, for Freckles. Mr. Wong is always taking Moti out, or bringing me leftovers. Watering my plants. I wanted to do something nice for him. I used to be quite handy. But I didn't consider the fact that I'd have to kneel on the floor to build the darn thing!"

"I can help!" Out of all the subjects covered in STEM, engineering was Sutton's greatest weakness. She could use the practice. And maybe if she was busy building something, it would be easier to forget about Riley with her whole, happy family, or Luis palling around with his mom.

Mrs. B was sort of a mom-figure. That was enough. Wasn't it?

CHAPTER TWELVE

Luis

Luis's mom might have stayed inside, but her eyes were lasered on his back from the window as he walked from their little house to the sidewalk. He was an astronaut leaving the space station for the first time, tethered to safety by her gaze.

But the thing about a tether was that it would only let him go so far.

It was silly. He and his mom had walked together to the Ave a million times. Their house was in the perfect location—one block to school, two blocks to the library, three blocks to Queen Anne Avenue.

With everything so close, they didn't even need a car, which was good because his mom's ancient Honda was very close to death and only to be used when absolutely necessary.

With his mom at his side, walking to the shops never felt like a space walk. Even as he turned at the corner to wave at her in the window, Luis expected her to burst out and insist she come along. But she didn't.

No sooner was Luis out of sight of his house than he stumbled upon his first obstacle: Mrs. Caliri's garden. Mrs. Caliri was a high-powered executive at one of the tech companies in town. Whenever Luis saw her climbing out of her Prius, she was always wearing heels and a dark suit. But the rest of the time, she was in jeans and up to her elbows in the dirt of her garden. The garden was a thing to behold, all twisty vines and cheerful flowers mingled together with herbs and tomatoes—Luis imagined Mary Lennox's secret garden must have looked exactly like this one, except there was no wall around this one.

This was nice for the neighbors who walked by and appreciated its splendor without fear of death. But for Luis, it was difficult to see beyond all the pollinators bustling around, attracted by the explosion of fragrant herbs and flowers. Closest to the sidewalk, a row of lavender bushes was in full bloom, chock-full of buzzing bees.

Luis knew this was a test. Heroes were always tested early in their journeys. When Penelope Bell first arrived at the Whitlow School for Extraordinary Children, she wasn't even allowed to enter the school grounds until she'd gotten past a gryphon. Which had been tricky, because Penelope hadn't yet realized the full extent of her powers.

But then, Luis figured, neither had he.

The easiest thing would be to cross the road and walk past on the other sidewalk. Luis didn't think the bees would chase him. It wasn't that kind of test. But he would have to backtrack to the corner so he wouldn't be jaywalking, and if his mom was still watching from the window, she would see him. And worry. Maybe even rethink her decision to let him go alone.

And she was almost definitely still watching.

Luis took another step toward the lavender bushes. It might have been his imagination, but he was almost certain the buzzing got more frantic. He faltered. But he was determined to succeed on this first hurdle. There would be many more to come. It wouldn't be a quest if it were simple!

And something else: At the Whitlow School for Extraordinary Children, the motto inscribed on the school crest was, "Courage is being afraid and charging forth regardless!"

Luis took a deep breath. People who say bees will only sting if they fear aggression have clearly never been rushed to the emergency room while losing feeling in their arms and legs. He took a step, and then two more, and then, in an unfortunate bit of neglect to street maintenance, an uneven part of the sidewalk where a giant root had broken through leaped up and made a sort of craggy hill out of the otherwise flat cement.

Luis went sprawling and maybe yelped a little, and as he went down, he knocked into the lavender bushes. The bees went up in an agitated swarm, their morning meal of lavender pollen disturbed.

Luis huddled on the sidewalk, terrified they would instead decide to make a meal of him (even though he knew bees didn't use their stingers to eat, but now was not the time to worry about mixed metaphors). When he did not feel any sharp pains and still had sensation in his arms and legs, he peeked his head up.

Some of the bees had resettled on the lavender. Some had moved over to the hydrangea bush. Luis grinned. Sure, his hands were a little skinned. But he had passed his first test.

His next test was even easier. Though it was tricky—it was the kind of obstacle that seemed enticing, completely not dangerous. But it had the potential to completely do the hero in. Like the field of poppies in *The Wizard of Oz*. (They were beautiful flowers! How could they do harm? And then, next thing you know, Dorothy and her friends were headed for an eternal snooze.)

Luis's obstacle also involved flowers. He wasn't allergic to flowers or grasses or anything that grew (except peanuts), but his allergies meant his immune system was a little too excitable. It would react to the slightest provocation, and the wrong kind of pollen up his nose could send him into a sneezing fit that would have his mother hovering until high school graduation.

At this moment, the challenge to Luis's excitable

immune system was a dandelion. But not the yellow ones Luis had made into a flower chain bracelet when he was in kindergarten (which was how he learned what happened when he spent too much time with dandelions). This was a dandelion that had turned into the white, puffy cloud part. It looked so comforting and inviting.

This particular dandelion was in the hand of a toddler out for a stroll with his dad. The toddler was puffing up his cheeks, preparing for that most terrifying of assaults. Luis watched it happen in slow motion—the toddler let out a gust of breath, and the tiny little seedpods of the dandelion poof exploded into the air, dancing on the wind and heading straight for Luis!

The child's father, completely oblivious to Luis's predicament, crowed and cheered, praising the little boy for the extraordinary job he had done of breathing (though to be fair, in Luis's experience, breathing was not always a simple matter).

What would Penelope Bell do? When spies from the Alistair Academy for Superior Children infiltrated the Whitlow School and tried to dose the Whitlow flyster team with a sleeping potion on the morning of the championships, Penelope had tricked them into dosing their own pomegranate juice. (She wouldn't have dosed the opposing team, as that would have been poor sportsmanship, but she had no qualms about dosing their spies and leaving them in a supply closet during the match.)

But a sleeping potion wasn't going to protect Luis from dandelion seeds. In the split second remaining before he would almost certainly inhale them, Luis pulled the neck of his shirt up over his face, to right beneath his eyes. Then he ran.

He couldn't swerve around the toddler and his father, because to one side was the Hoppers' ferocious dog—behind a fence, but still—and to the other was the street. (A super narrow, extremely unbusy street, but it would be just Luis's luck to run into the street at the exact moment a car finally came rolling by.)

So he barreled through, right in between the man yelling, "Yes, Aidan, good job! Good blowing!" and the little boy gearing up to blow again. It was a risk, and there were consequences. Luis felt the boy reach out and brush his dandelion-covered hand against Luis's pant leg as he passed by. But contamination or not, he got past.

He ran all the way to the end of the block. And then he was at Queen Anne Avenue, and the corner store was to his left. A bounty of fresh markers awaited!

He'd still have to brave the return trip, of course. But for now this hero would enjoy his well-deserved reward.

CHAPTER THIRTEEN

Sutton

Cat condos, as it turned out, were harder to build than Sutton had expected. She hoped Freckles and Mr. Wong would like it, if she ever managed to finish. It certainly gave her a new appreciation for the kids who did engineering projects at the All-State Science Fair. She'd always considered those projects little more than glorified LEGO creations, but she saw now how wrong she'd been.

"I need two more of these connector thingies," Sutton said from behind the couch, where she was scavenging for scattered pieces. She popped up a hand to show Mrs. B what she meant. "Do you see them?"

"Oh! Over by the TV! I see one!"

As Sutton crawled over to the TV, Moti scampered through the collection of tubes and connectors on the floor, scattering them yet again. Sutton took a deep breath. She loved Moti, but there was a reason great scientists didn't keep dogs around their labs.

"You okay, my dear? You look like you've got a lot on your mind. And not only the cat condo. Is this about your mom?"

Sutton shook her head vehemently and consulted the plans. She'd already put together several cubes with the tubes and connectors, and she'd hung little hammocks inside the cubes. Now she needed to make a sort of pyramid thing that went on top and required this one funny connector that was different from the others.

"You know what?" Mrs. B went on while Sutton searched for the connector. "I think you and your dad have the most special relationship. I know how hard it is to be far away from your parents."

Sutton found the connector and focused on the task at hand. Everyone thought they knew how she felt, but no one really did. People thought she wanted her mom around for the big things, like birthdays and science fairs. And she did. But mostly she wanted her mom around for morning hot chocolate and walking Moti, and drifting off to sleep while listening to the sound of her mom's typing.

"Does she tell you much about her work? Are they making any new penguin discoveries?"

Sutton sighed. "The migration patterns are changing. Because of melting ice. If there's not enough ice, or if there's too much, the conditions aren't right to hatch their eggs. So they have to find new breeding grounds."

"You're so smart. All I know about penguins is they mate for life!"

Sutton didn't bother telling Mrs. B this wasn't actually true of emperor penguins. It was such a common misconception; it was like the number of people who thought being homeschooled meant she never interacted with any other children. One of the librarians at her local branch was always drinking out of a mug with two penguins gazing adoringly at each other inside a heart, and the words, YOU'RE MY PENGUIN.

A lot of species of penguins choose partners

and stick with them for the rest of their lives, like getting married and living happily ever after. But not all marriages last for happily ever after. And emperor penguins get new mates each breeding season.

The one thing people usually got right about emperors was how the dads care for the chicks while the mom is away. The focus was usually on how cool that was, what great dads the penguins are. Which is true. But no one ever commented on how when the moms return, the dads leave. Emperor families are, by design, never together.

"Did you ever live far away from your family?" Sutton asked.

"I did. My baba left India first, to come to the United States and get settled—find a job, find a place for us to live. My brother followed a couple of years later, so I was separated from him, too. Then, when it was time for me to go to college, my mother and I traveled to the United States and we all lived together again. Of course, then we were far away from all the family we'd left behind in India."

Sutton had almost finished assembling the pyramid part. There was something really satisfying about engineering—the results of her work were coming to life right in front of her. If the pieces didn't fit together correctly, she could see it right away and try again with a different approach. "Who did you leave behind?"

"I had two older sisters who were already married, and they stayed with their new families. Some cousins are still there. My grandmother came over about a year after we did."

Mrs. B looked very far away, but she and Sutton were both yanked back to the present when Moti leapt off the couch, skidded across the coffee table, and scattered the building plans on her way to the sliding door.

"Moti!" Sutton threw her body in front of the in-process cat condo before Moti could run straight through it.

Mrs. B chuckled. "Would you open the sliding door, dear? You know how Moti and Freckles refuse to be kept apart."

Sure enough, there was Freckles on the other side of the glass, waiting patiently while Moti boinged in front of the door like she was on a trampoline. As soon as Sutton cracked the door open, Moti shot out onto the balcony, then herded Freckles inside.

Mrs. Banerjee reached for her phone. "I'll

let Mr. Wong know Freckles is here." As Mrs. B texted, Sutton thought about a younger version of her neighbor saying goodbye to her father as he went off to a country she couldn't even imagine. Maybe Mrs. B really did understand how she felt. And when Mrs. B was a teenager, there wouldn't have been any Internet.

"How did you stay in contact with your dad and your brother? And your family in India once you were here? Because you couldn't email, right? Or video chat, or . . ."

Mrs. Banerjee laughed. "Oh, we managed to get along in the dark ages before the Internet. But it was hard. We wrote letters—real ones, on paper, with stamps!—and they took a long time to travel across oceans. We made occasional phone calls, though they were very expensive and we paid by the minute, so they were always rushed. Ultimately, I guess, we relied on our memories, and our love, and the knowledge that we would be together again eventually."

A few years ago, Sutton's grandmother had given her some stationery—with penguins, of course—and Sutton had buried it in the back of her closet with the rest of the penguin junk people gave her. Who was she going to write a letter to, anyway? But maybe she would dig it out. She didn't know how many stamps it would take for a letter to get to Antarctica. Probably so many they would cover the envelope.

"You look like you need some golden milk," Mrs. Banerjee said.

Sutton left the cat condo half-built and went to sit next to her on the couch. "I think I need to learn how to make it," she said. "Can you give me instructions from here? I'm super careful with the stove."

Mrs. Banerjee put her arm around Sutton and held her close for a minute. "I think that's a wonderful idea."

Sutton followed Mrs. B's instructions step by step; cooking was basically science too. She warmed the milk and measured out the spices and drizzled the honey. She was slowly pouring the steaming yellow liquid into mugs when a knock at the door startled her. A few drops splattered onto the counter as Sutton's dad poked his head in.

"How are my two favorite ladies?" he said. He was super sweaty from his run, and he had this goofy grin on his face that he'd had a lot lately, ever since he started dating Elizabeth.

And Sutton couldn't help but wonder—was it

true? Were she and Mrs. B still his two favorite ladies? After her dad came home early from that fancy date, he'd never made a big announcement. But he probably hadn't had enough time to go through with whatever he was planning before Elizabeth's son had his allergic reaction. Sutton had seen her dad with Elizabeth at the MoPOP, heads close together, hand gentle on the small of her back. She was definitely moving up the ranks of favorite ladies.

"We're doing all right, dear," Mrs. B said. "I don't know how I'd get by without Sutton here."

Maybe Mrs. B was only saying that. Or maybe she really needed her. But it was starting to seem like her dad was doing fine without her.

CHAPTER FOURTEEN

Luis

The sniffling started before Luis even got home from the corner store.

He did his best to hide it from his mom as she hovered over him. She kept her hands in her pockets, and part of Luis wondered if she had an EpiPen lurking there in the folds of her skirt, in case she needed to jab him in the thigh with lifesaving medicine on a moment's notice.

"I'm fine, Mom," he said. And he was. It was only sniffles—he hoped. "I got my markers! I'm going to go work on my book, okay?"

They weren't very good markers—his mom had been right about that. The convenience store had a terrible selection of art supplies. But that hadn't really been the point. He'd gone on a (mini) quest and been successful! The ideas for Penelope's next adventure were starting to flow. He'd gotten unstuck!

He sniffled and then froze, wishing he'd been able to control his nose until he'd reached his bedroom.

"Luis?"

Oh no. If she thought his quest had made him sick, his mom would never let him leave the house again. But all his writing inspiration was out there in the outside world. He couldn't create something great and full of adventure if he was always stuck inside!

She came over and took his face in her hands. He tensed and prepared himself for all the reasons he could never leave the house alone again. Instead, she kissed him on the forehead. "You're getting so grown up," she said. "I'll try not to get in the way too much. I just worry."

Luis hugged her tight. Of course she worried. He worried too. But he was done letting it keep him from adventures—his own or Penelope's.

The trouble was, before he could figure out how Penelope and her friends were going to expose their Alistair Academy foes' newest dastardly plans, Luis was in full-blown immune-system freak-out. It wasn't an emergency room situation. It was a tissues/allergy medicine/humidifier situation. But it was impossible to hide from his mom. Especially after he sneezed six times in a row.

"It might just be a cold," he said when she appeared in his doorway, holding the fizzy vitamin C drink he downed by the gallon during cold-and-flu season. She pursed her lips; she didn't believe that. Neither did he. But he took the drink and smiled like he believed.

It wasn't enough. She crossed her arms and gave him The Look. The Look that meant you better get in bed right now, mister, or we will have words once the swelling has gone down enough for you to pay attention.

Luis took a gulp of the drink, then sank into his bed. His mom nodded like she'd won that battle and pulled his door mostly shut behind her. Not all the way shut, though. She would be listening.

It was funny—the first time Luis had a peanut reaction at school, his mom was ready to pull him out and move them to a completely sealed-off house in the middle of nowhere. Luis had argued—with help from his grandparents—that he loved school; and Queen Anne Hill; and their cozy, cluttered little house; and he could go to school and be safe if he was careful. He didn't want to live in a bubble that kept him away from the world.

Sometimes he felt like he was trapped inside a bubble anyway—moving through the world, maybe, but not able to really reach out and touch anything. But Penelope Bell could. She was unstoppable.

Luis hopped from bed and reached for his notebook—new ideas were flowing and he had to get them on paper. He miscalculated a little, considering his fuzzy allergy brain, and crashed into his desk.

"Luis!" His mom was back in the doorway so quickly, Luis was almost sure she'd been camped out in the hallway. "Are you all right? What happened?"

Luis reached out to steady a stack of books threatening to topple over, then turned around slowly. "I wanted to work on my book?"

In an unfortunate bit of timing—all of it had been unfortunate, really—he then sneezed so hard that his knees buckled, and Mom hustled forward, shoving him into bed less gently than seemed reasonable if she thought he was so sick.

"You are staying in bed," she said. "And I am going to make grilled cheese sandwiches. Then we are going to watch movies together for the rest of the day, do you understand me, Luisito?"

They wouldn't really be grilled cheese sandwiches, though. The cheese-like ingredient would be made from rice milk. The gluten-free bread was basically cardboard.

But his mom was the real deal, and that was never going to change.

Once Luis heard her clanking around in the kitchen, he moved much more carefully and retrieved his notebook and his new pack of markers. The rice milk cheese took forever to melt, so he figured he had a good twenty minutes before the food was ready. That should be enough time to jot down all the ideas rocketing through his brain before she came back and made him rest.

"You have such an extraordinary imagination," Luis's mom said to him at bedtime, after he'd told her the latest in Penelope's adventures. "You definitely get that from your dad, not me."

Luis knew his dad had been an artist; one of his paintings even hung in the living room. But he wondered if he got his writing from his dad. "Did he tell stories?"

"Not like you do, but when we first met, he was always drawing comics. There's a box of his sketchbooks around here somewhere. You remind me of him when you're scribbling away in a notebook." She kissed his forehead and turned out the light. "Sleep tight, love."

Luis was exhausted. But even though he had been dozing off during the last movie of their marathon, suddenly he was wide-awake. His dad had been an artist. Not only that, but there were sketchbooks somewhere in the house.

→ CHAPTER FIFTEEN

Sutton

After his shower the next morning, Sutton's dad appeared in her bedroom doorway. He clapped his hands and rubbed them together like he was dreaming up some sort of wild, exciting plan. But really it was the same plan as every Sunday.

"Farmers' market! Let's roll, my favorite offspring!"

Sutton rolled her eyes, but she also sprang out the door ahead of her father. The South Lake Union Sunday Farmers' Market was one of her favorite places, despite its location in the out-of-doors.

For one thing, the guy at the bakery booth always saved broken cookie pieces for her.

They stopped by Mrs. B's apartment before they left to see if she needed anything. She was right where they'd left her, on the couch, with an ice pack on her knee.

"Why don't you come stay with us for a few days?" Sutton's dad said. "You can have my room, and I'll crash on the couch. That way we can make sure you're taken care of."

"But then I'll feel like a decrepit old lady," she said, pulling Moti into her lap. "You are very sweet, Martin, but it's not as serious as all that. You two go enjoy this glorious day! We haven't had one like this in ages!"

"Oh, Seattle," Sutton's dad chuckled. "We've got to soak up every minute of sun, right?"

Sutton sighed on her way out the door. There was no point in telling her dad what she'd already told him a bunch of times. On average there were 152 sunny days per year in Seattle. More than 40 percent! And a whole bunch of cities got way more rain each year than Seattle, like Philadelphia, Boston, Atlanta, Houston, and Miami! But when it was sunny in Miami, people probably didn't shake their heads and say, "Gosh, we better go soak up that rare Miami sun!"

It was a short walk to the farmers' market, where, rain or shine, the vendors set up their vegetables and fruits, plants and pastries. Botany wasn't Sutton's primary scientific interest, but she always enjoyed chatting with the farmers about how the weather had affected their crops, or how heirloom seeds produced a different sort of plant than hybrids, and what different fertilizers did to soil.

"Shall we divide and conquer?" her dad asked, looking over his list. "I get veggies, you get fruits, we meet at pastries?"

Sutton surveyed the maze of stands and walkways before them. She'd walked these aisles alone dozens of times. She would never get stuck like her bot, endlessly spinning around, unsure which way to turn. But something in her didn't want to risk it.

She grabbed her dad's hand. "Let's stick together today."

"Righty-o! A united front!"

It took three different stands to get all the veggies on the list. They were heading toward Sutton's favorite plant vendor when a busker called out, "Hey, Martin!"

Sutton's dad went to talk to the fiddler sitting on the sidewalk next to his open case, which held scattered coins and a few dollar bills. He looked sort of familiar, but her dad knew so many musicians around town that Sutton had no idea where this guy was from. She hung back, counting her money and figuring out if she had enough to buy the *Orchidaceae* plant she'd been saving up for.

She couldn't ignore it when the fiddler waved his bow at her, though.

"Hey there! Sutton, right?"

She nodded and stepped closer to her dad.

"What instrument do you play?"

"The keyboard," she said with a sly grin at her dad. It was their little joke. Whenever she was coding at the computer, she told him she was playing the keyboard, making her own kind of music.

"Awesome!" the fiddler said. "I bet you're chock-full of talent. With a dad like yours, you've got to be musical!"

When her dad bid his friend goodbye (tossing a few bills in the case as he went), they headed toward Sutton's favorite plant stand.

"I have enough to get the *Cymbidium Orchidaceae*, if Mr. Garcia still has it this week."

"You know," her dad said, "if you ever wanted to learn how to play the real keyboard . . ."

"I do play the real keyboard."

Sutton liked music okay. There was a lot of math involved. She loved listening to her dad make music, even if she didn't really love listening to the whole orchestra. And she admired musicians and how hard they worked to master their instruments. But she had never, ever felt the desire to learn an instrument herself.

"Señorita Sutton!" boomed Mr. Garcia as they appeared at his booth. "*Cymbidium Orchidaceae*, ¿sí?"

He led her to the delicate orchids arranged in the back of the booth, away from the curious hands of toddlers who might snap off a bud without realizing how much care and patience these finicky flowers required. Mr. Garcia went over orchid care at length, as though Sutton hadn't been researching it for months already.

Finally she thanked him and they were on their way. After visits to the fruit, cheese, and sausage vendors, Sutton and her dad arrived at Just Desserts, where Mr. Calvin handed over a bag of broken cookie pieces with a big wink. "You get what you pay for," he said, like he always said.

It wasn't true. If she truly got what she paid for, she wouldn't get anything. He gave the broken pieces away. But she wasn't about to correct him.

Her dad paid for several pastries and was trying to figure out how to carry all the bags and also eat a bear claw while they walked back to their apartment, when another voice called out.

"Martin? Martin Jensen?"

Sutton didn't know how people were always recognizing her dad, considering he sat in the third row of the enormous orchestra with his cello. From the look on her dad's face, he sort of recognized the approaching woman, but couldn't place how he knew her.

"Oh, Martin, how great to run into you! And look at your little one! She's not a toddler anymore!"

Sutton bristled. She was almost ten. And tall for her age.

But the woman still felt the need to lean over with her hands on her knees, so her face was right in Sutton's face.

"What's your name again, honey?"

"Sutton," she said. Then she took pity on her dad, who still seemed completely lost, and added, "What's yours?"

"Oh, Sutton!" the woman said, speaking to her dad as though Sutton wasn't there. "That's right! I loved how you guys used Julie's maiden name for the baby's first name. So clever. Gender neutral." Then as an afterthought, she said to Sutton, "My name's Felicia, honey. Your mom and I were in a new-moms group together when you were tiny!"

"So good to see you again, Felicia," Sutton's dad said.

"Where's Julie today?"

Her dad opened his mouth to answer, then closed it again, like the koi in the pond outside the pediatrician's office. Her parents had been divorced for so many years that people rarely asked. People in their neighborhood just knew it was Sutton and her dad, her dad and Sutton.

While he looked for a diplomatic way to respond, Sutton took matters into her own hands. "Julie's at the South Pole," she said. "Nice to see you, Felicia." Then she dragged her dad toward home.

CHAPTER SIXTEEN

Luis

After a restless night imagining what he might find in his dad's sketchbooks, Luis was up early the next morning. He didn't want to wake his mom, who had been giggling on the phone until late into the night, so he crept as quietly as he could out to the garage.

There was exactly enough room for the battered old Honda, and all around it, artfully stacked, were boxes and piles of stuff. He didn't even know what it all was. He usually avoided the garage entirely and waited in the driveway for his mom to pull the car out.

There were boxes labeled BABY CLOTHES and FINAN-CIAL and one labeled CHINA, which Luis assumed meant fancy dishes, but his brain started to dance down a path where his mom had spent some part of her life in China and kept the memories of those weeks or months or years in that box in the garage.

Not everything was organized in boxes. A broken Crock-Pot, a shopping bag full of mismatched shoes, a winter sled, and an old-fashioned-looking steamer trunk were balanced in an artful pile. An exercise bike, several cracked and empty flowerpots, the car seat Luis outgrew years ago, and the crutches his mom needed when she sprained her ankle last fall made up another pile. At the top of that pile, Luis saw his treasure—a box labeled MATEO.

He'd once asked his mom what was in that box with his dad's name on it, and she'd said old papers. But sketchbooks were paper.

The box was not, however, within reach. The exercise bike was tipped on its end, about as tall as Luis himself. He could reach the car seat and flower-pots where they were jumbled atop the bike, and the tips of his fingers could barely graze the bottom of the crutches, if he really stretched.

By using the box by his feet as a stepstool, he was

tall enough to get a hand around the bottom of one of the crutches. And jostling the crutch should be enough to loosen the box he wanted and drop it into his arms.

It seemed like a good plan. Sort of. It seemed like a plan, anyway.

He stepped on the box, reached past the bike and the pots and the car seat, wrapped a hand around the crutch to jostle it—okay so far—and then it all went wrong.

His foot crashed through the box he was standing on. He lost his balance and went flying backward, his grip still strong on the crutch, as though it might somehow keep him upright even though it was also falling through the air. And then he was not only on his back, but an avalanche of stuff was falling down on top of him.

"Luis!"

His mom was in the doorway, her hair a wild halo, all giddiness from her evening chat with Martin washed away in an instant of terror.

It took a lot longer to get out of the pile of stuff than it had taken to get covered by it. And as soon as Mom realized Luis was actually unharmed, her concern turned to irritation, which built into something closer to fury as she untangled the mess.

"What were you thinking . . . could have been killed . . . almost had a heart attack . . . think before you act . . . just ask for help . . ."

Luis's head spun. Dizzy, he sank back down to sit on the concrete stairs leading into the kitchen. "I wanted to see Papi's sketchbooks," he said, trying desperately not to burst into tears. "I'm sorry. I'll clean all this up."

"Don't be sorry," she said, her face softening. "At least not about wanting to see the sketchbooks. You should have just asked for help. We'll deal with the mess together, since it's my fault there's so much junk out here to begin with. But first, let's find what you were looking for."

The MATEO box had been among the things that had crashed down on top of Luis when he'd fallen. His mom dragged it over, reached in, and pulled out a picture frame, the glass broken. Underneath the jagged edges stood Luis's father with his older brother and sister, all of them teenagers.

The tears Luis had been holding back burst forth. "I'm so sorry!"

His mother reached out and pulled him close. "Oh, love, it's okay. Look, the photograph is fine.

We'll get a new frame. Plus, it's been sitting out here in a box. The best photos are all inside, displayed."

That was true. There were photos of Papi all over the house. Still. "Can I have this one?"

"Of course." His mom carefully removed the photo from the broken frame and handed it over. "You can have any of this stuff." She sifted through a few more things in the box and pulled out a yellowed piece of paper. "Look at this."

Luis's eyes were drawn first to the official-looking seal in the top left corner with the same long-tailed bird that was on all the Guatemalan handicrafts around their house. The words on the page were Spanish, which Luis's mom had learned when she lived with his dad in Guatemala after college. When his dad died, she'd kept speaking it with Luis at home, at least sometimes. So he understood a lot, and spoke some, but reading it was harder. He wrapped his mouth around the words slowly.

"'El Registrador Civil de la capital certifica . . . ,'" he read.

His mom kissed the top of his head. "It's your papi's birth certificate." She kept digging through the box to see what else she might discover. There was a notepad filled with batting lineups for the softball team his dad used to coach. His Guatemalan passport. And finally, a stack of battered sketchbooks. She handed one to Luis and opened one herself.

Luis hugged his close to his chest. For some reason, he wanted to look at it later, when he was alone. His mom traced her fingers over the page in front of her. "He really was talented," she murmured.

But then something in the box caught her eye. "Oh!" She brought it out reverently. "I remember this. . . ."

At first Luis thought it was a pocket watch, but when she flipped open the bronze cover, he saw something else: a compass. A shiver went down his spine. It looked like something Penelope Bell would find in the off-limits attic of the Whitlow School, a magical object that would have the power to help her defeat evil.

"That was Papi's?"

She nodded and handed the compass to Luis. He had held things that belonged to his dad before. But this felt somehow different. Magical. Like it held a little piece of his soul. A horcrux, but in a good way.

"What did he use a compass for?"

Luis's mom ran her fingers back and forth across his back. It almost tickled, but didn't. "Your abuelos gave that compass to him when he left Guatemala for the United States."

Luis had heard stories of the immigrants who came from Central America, all the way across Mexico by land, through deserts and dangers. It wasn't an exciting journey, like a quest in a story, either.

"I thought Papi came here on an airplane."

His mom smiled. "He did. His family saved and saved, and his great-aunt in Los Angeles sponsored him. He came to finish high school in the United States." Mom took the compass back, cradling it carefully in her hands. "The compass was really a symbol," she said. "So he could always find his way home. To Guatemala."

"His home was here, though. With you. With us." At least, it had been for the short time Luis had had with his father, which hadn't been long enough.

"It was. But it was also Guatemala. And he did go home! We visited a few times."

Luis didn't really remember, but there were pictures on the mantel from a trip when he'd been around two, shortly before his dad got cancer. Holding his abuela's hand as they walked through an open-air market. Arms tight around his abuelo as they rode together in the back of a tuk tuk—a tiny three-wheeled taxi of sorts. Learning to make tortillas with his mom.

"You should have this," she said, pressing the compass back into his hands. "To help you find your way."

"To where, though?" Luis tried to ignore the magic tingle in the palm of his hand. The compass called to him, but what was the point? He didn't need to find his way back home. He never left home.

"To wherever you want to go," his mother said. "I'm sorry if I've made you feel like you're stuck, like the outside world is dangerous. Sure, there are dangers. Maybe a few more for you than for other people. But you have an explorer's spirit, love." She pressed a kiss to his forehead. "Let's explore."

CHAPTER SEVENTEEN

Sutton

"And then her mouth snapped shut like one of those koi fish at Swansons Nursery!"

"Sutton, honey . . ."

Dad's voice had a warning edge to it, but the corners of his lips were quirking up. Aunt Lindsay was over for Sunday-night dinner and Sutton had been regaling her with the story of the nosy lady at the farmers' market since she arrived. It was funnier now that they were home.

Aunt Lindsay grinned. "Sounds like you told her what's what." She turned to Sutton's dad. "How about you, little brother? Are you still seeing the scientist? What was her name?"

"Elizabeth," Sutton mumbled.

"Elizabeth, yes. In fact . . ."

His voice trailed off in a troublesome way. *In fact, we're getting married? In fact, we're hoping Sutton can live with you while we travel the world together? In fact, we're having a baby of our own?*

"Don't keep us in suspense," Aunt Lindsay said.

"Oh, it's not a big deal. Just that Liz and I were talking, and we want to try another family date. The MoPOP maybe wasn't quite fair. It was somewhere Luis was comfortable, but you weren't, pumpkin. So we want to try again on neutral ground."

Sutton stared at her plate. This was better than some of the other things he could have said. But he had definitely brought this up in front of Aunt Lindsay on purpose, so he'd have backup if Sutton freaked out.

"So . . . we were thinking about a hike in Discovery Park!"

Aunt Lindsay snorted. But when he said nothing more, she said, "Wait, you're serious? A hike?"

Sutton's thoughts exactly. If they were going for somewhere Sutton would be comfortable, a hike was the worst possible idea! What next? A Mariners game? An improv class?

"Sure. Liz and I have been on quite a few hikes together now. We thought it would be a fun thing to share with the kids."

Sutton exchanged a glance with Aunt Lindsay. Aunt Lindsay once went "camping" to a place with room service, Wi-Fi, a Jacuzzi, and a butler, and she still complained about the bugs.

Sutton's dad busied himself with pouring cream into a fresh cup of coffee.

"So is this serious, Martin?" Lindsay asked, breaking the awkward silence. "You're spending time with each other's kids?"

"You know me, Linds. I'm never serious." Sutton's dad made a goofy face and then looked pointedly at the dishes. "Clear the table, hon, and then maybe your aunt can help you figure out the glitch in your robot."

"Pretty sure your daughter is way smarter than I am at this point," Lindsay said.

"You built an electric guitar when you were her age!" her brother pointed out.

"I peaked early." Lindsay stood up to help Sutton clear the dishes, ignoring her brother's grunt of protest.

"It's okay," Sutton said. Time with Aunt Lindsay was too precious to spend on the bot, which she was unlikely to be able to help with. Aunt Lindsay was more tech-savvy than Sutton's dad, but only a little. Just enough so that she could keep up with her middle school students. "Let's just do the dishes."

"What do you hear from your mom?" Lindsay asked once they were both in the kitchen.

"Not much."

"I got an email from her a few days ago." Lindsay rummaged in the cupboards for containers to hold the leftovers.

Sutton said nothing. There was nothing to say without betraying how upset she was about her birthday, how terrified she was that Elizabeth would tear her father away and Sutton would have no one. If she opened her mouth, a whole world of feelings would spew out. It would be too messy.

Sutton focused on the mess in front of her instead, rinsing gunk off dishes and setting them in the dishwasher.

"She's really disappointed she won't be home for your birthday."

Sutton harrumphed. Aunt Lindsay had always been a neat link between her parents—her dad's sister and her mom's best friend. Her presence in their lives had always made Sutton feel like they were all still a family, even though her parents were divorced. But Sutton didn't want to hear her aunt defend her mom.

Once the dishes were done, Sutton left her dad and Aunt Lindsay to their hushed conversation—probably about Elizabeth, and Sutton really didn't want to know—and retreated to her room.

She searched through the back of her closet until she found the set of penguin stationery from her grandparents. Sutton wasn't sure she'd ever written a letter on paper. She wasn't sure she'd even send this one. But this is what she wrote:

Dear Mom,

I know you're not going to be home for my birthday. And you'll probably be home before this letter reaches Antarctica. I could email you, but I guess I kind of want to have something that feels sure and certain. A piece of paper I can touch and send through the mail, and know you'll touch it too. Eventually.

I don't want to make you feel bad. I know your work is important. But I'm important too.

I don't need a lot of people in my life. I don't even <u>want</u> a lot of people in my life. But right now it feels like the two people I want most are slipping away.

We're supposed to be a family, in our own weird way. But right now it feels like we're three different bots, all bouncing off the walls in different parts of the same maze. Something's gone wrong with our code, and I don't know how to fix it.

Your daughter,
Sutton, almost 10

CHAPTER EIGHTEEN

Luis

Luis began his Monday morning by sitting on his bed with his dad's sketchbook, poring over the pages with his heart thumping a drumbeat in his chest. Some of the sketches were in the familiar style of his dad's art that hung around the house—bold lines and shapes that looked abstract, but if you looked more closely, figures started to emerge. People, animals, landscapes. Luis loved the style, but he didn't see a story in it.

Other pages were filled with comic-style characters—superheroes, fairies, dragons, trees with faces, centaurs, robots. Anything and everything, really. Sometimes there'd be one sketch of a character and it wouldn't appear again in the sketchbook. But other characters reappeared, and developed over the pages, and eventually spoke to one another in multi-panel comics.

His dad had been good. Really, really good. Luis wasn't sure his own storytelling could ever live up to his father's artistic skill.

But he was also excited to try.

Then his mom had told him they were going to see Sutton and her dad again. Luis had been filled with dread; the MoPOP hadn't exactly gone well. He barely had time to process the idea of another encounter with Sutton before his mom told him what they were going to do that day: a hike.

A hike.

Now he sat in the back seat, his emotions even more jumbled because the car wouldn't start. He waited as his mom ran to see if Mrs. Springer next door could help.

If they could get the car started, they were going on a hike through Discovery Park—534 acres, twelve miles of trails, and a 100 percent chance of bees. There was some trepidation at this revelation, but mostly Luis was elated. Sure, Mom would be right there every step of the way with her anti-allergy emergency kit. She'd made that clear when she'd laid out all the steps they would take in every possible catastrophe. She'd even made him demonstrate his use of the practice EpiPen (which thankfully didn't have a needle in it).

But still! This felt like she really meant it when she said she was going to try to loosen up and let him experience more things.

And then they'd gotten in the car, and it had made that horrible chugga-chugga sound it made when it decided it needed a break.

His mom came back with Mrs. Springer—a children's book author who was always wearing pajamas and loved talking to Luis about what he was reading. They had this down to a system. Mrs. Springer pulled her car around so it was nose-to-nose with the ancient Honda. Both women popped the hoods on their cars, and Luis's mom attached cables from one battery to the other. Then Mrs. Springer got back in her car and turned its engine on.

This was when the magic happened.

Of course, it wasn't really magic—more like the mechanics of how car engines work—but it sparked an idea. Penelope Bell and her friends at the Whitlow School could use Marjorie's power of conducting electricity through her fingers to power the broken-down airship when they needed to rush to stop the Dark Force in its dastardly tracks.

Luis dug out the notebook he'd packed into his backpack and jotted down these thoughts.

With her car still attached to Mrs. Springer's engine, Mom got back in and tried her engine again. As though Marjorie had touched it with her electric fingers, it sprang to life. Mom waved to Mrs. Springer, and Luis rolled down his window.

"Thank you!" he called.

"You're welcome! You two call me if you get stranded somewhere!"

She was trying to be nice. But a seed of worry had been planted, and Luis couldn't keep it from springing up into a tiny plant.

"What if we do?" he said. "Get stranded."

What he didn't say was: *What if we go on this hike and a bee stings me and we can't get to a hospital because the car won't start?* The thing was, if he was thinking it, his mom had already thought it. Hadn't she? Usually she worried enough for the both of them. Though maybe she was so la-la over Sutton's dad, she wasn't thinking straight.

Luis was the one who thought in curvy lines and patterns and mazes. He needed his mom to think straight.

"The car's running now," she said. "It'll get us to the park fine. And if we have any trouble leaving the park, Martin will be there."

Right. Martin and Sutton. Sutton, who was probably an expert in how a car engine worked. Not that she'd want to tell him anything about it. Every time he'd tried to talk to her, she'd clammed up. Shy was one thing, but she had clearly not been happy to be at the MoPOP. Who can't have fun at a museum full of superheroes, science fiction, and fantasy?

Still, Luis was determined to give Sutton another chance, for his mom. She'd been so happy since she started going on dates with Martin. Not that she'd been unhappy before, but now she sang while she made dinner and made goofy faces at her phone while texting, and she had loosened up enough to bring Luis on a hike!

He closed his eyes and let the music distract him—mostly. It was *Into the Woods*, a Broadway musical about a bunch of fairy-tale characters going into the woods on a quest. That was his mom's sense of humor.

Probably she hadn't been thinking ahead to the part of the musical where the giant comes down the beanstalk and tramples the woods and kills Jack's mother and the Baker's wife.

His eyes still closed, Luis felt the car swerve off the main road. "Are we almost there?"

"Yes, love," his mom said from the front seat. "We have our plan, right?"

"We stick together. You carry the Benadryl, I carry the EpiPen—"

"And if we get separated, meet in the parking lot," his mom finished. "But we don't need to worry, because we're going to be together the whole time." She pulled into a parking space and turned around in her seat. "I think this will be good. Sutton will open up. Let's give her a chance."

It wasn't like Luis really had an option. They were here. But he hoped his mom was right. If not, this was going to be a seriously long hike.

CHAPTER NINETEEN

Sutton

Sutton did not want to go hiking. But she was determined to make up for the MoPOP; she couldn't risk pushing her dad any further away. And if she was going, she was going to be prepared. She checked the battery on her tablet again: full. There were maps on there. And navigational tools. And survival information, if the worst should happen.

Sutton was pretty sure the worst would happen.

"Sutton, honey?"

She met her dad's eyes in the rearview mirror. "What?" It came out sharper than she meant it to.

But they were almost there. She needed to go over the route one more time.

"Promise you'll keep an open mind?"

Sutton nodded and followed the trail on her screen: through the park entrance, across a bridge, between two boulders, through a stream. . . .

Through a stream? How had she not noticed that before? Her dad had promised they would not get wet. She wanted him to be pleased with her attitude, but there were limits. Sutton pulled off her watch and stuffed it under the driver's seat in front of her. Just to be sure. The watch had a GPS system built in, plus it could tell the time in any time zone, give the weather forecast, and could probably make Sutton's bed, if she programmed it right. But the one thing it was *not*? Waterproof.

A few scattered cars dotted the parking lot. They pulled into a space near a cracked and faded map mounted under milky glass. Sutton hugged her tablet a little closer. Did anyone actually trust that map? It looked like it had been baking in the sun since before Sutton was born. A decade—maybe more!

Trusting a map that old was ridiculous. Nature was not fixed. It changed. Earthquakes and avalanches and floods. The globe got hotter every minute. That was why the emperor penguins had to find new migration routes. Whatever had been true when the map was first drawn couldn't still be true.

That was just science.

"There they are!" Sutton's dad pointed at a faded red car already parking in the lot. He twisted around in his seat to look at Sutton. "I'm really glad we're doing this, pumpkin."

Sutton nodded and slipped the tablet into its waterproof sleeve. She checked her backpack: rain gear, trail rations, water bottle, first aid kit, and bear spray.

"Are you sure you want to carry all that?" her dad asked. Again. "It's only going to be a couple of hours."

"I'm sure."

Sutton climbed out of the car and immediately wanted to dive back inside. Something buzzed around her head. The sun's rays would burn off the top level of her skin soon. But worst of all, she only had one bar of service on her tablet.

Her dad pulled a backpack half the size of Sutton's out of the car's trunk. He waved toward Elizabeth's battered car. "Good morning!"

From across the parking lot, a cheery voice said, "Morning! Hi, Sutton!"

But Sutton barely heard Elizabeth's sunny voice. If she lost service to her tablet, she wouldn't only lose the trail maps. She'd lose the app with the pictures of poisonous plants, the first aid app, the build-a-campfire app, and the build-a-shelter app. Also, she wouldn't have access to her coding program if making her way through the maze of woods gave her any great insights into programming her bot.

(Unlikely, but she was willing to take inspiration wherever it came.)

Then it happened. Her dad leaned down, took the tablet from her hands, and whispered in her ear, "Sutton, honey. People, not pixels."

She huffed, but made her best attempt to keep her frustration under control. She had an open mind! She was making an effort! Plus, if she pasted on a smile, made eye contact, and answered questions with multiple words, she usually got her device back. Although if there was no service, it wouldn't do her any good anyway.

"That's quite a full pack you've got there," Sutton's dad said to Luis. "Sutton likes to be prepared too."

Sutton peeked at Luis, who shifted his backpack on his skinny shoulders. It was full to bursting. Maybe he had a tablet in there.

"Like I told Sutton, it'll only take us a couple of hours to make the full loop."

Elizabeth laughed. "We've had the same talk. He's not leaving anything behind. How was your drive?"

The adults drifted over to the faded map near the trail entrance. Sutton fidgeted with the straps that hung off her backpack. She squeezed her eyes shut when her father pressed a kiss to Elizabeth's forehead.

"Science fiction can be based in real science," Luis blurted.

She turned away from their parents to look at him.

"It seemed like . . . at the MoPOP . . ." He trailed off, but then gathered his thoughts again. "Have you read *A Wrinkle in Time*? I read an interview with a scientist who said that tessering is seventy percent based in real science."

A Wrinkle in Time was sitting on Sutton's bookshelf—one of many books her dad had given her, hoping she'd read.

"Okay," she said. She'd never heard of tessering.

They both glanced over at their parents. Sutton's dad had his arm around Elizabeth. He pointed to something on the map with the other hand. She laughed softly.

"You should read it," Luis finally said.

"Okay." Sutton paused. Maybe she would. A story based mostly in real science might actually be interesting.

"All right, my friends." Sutton's dad turned toward them. "How about we get this hike started?"

There was no way out now. Sutton was going to spend the next two hours in the not-so-great outdoors. Maybe three, depending how quickly they walked. Three hours was hardly anything. She designed her first 2-D platform game in less time than that.

"I understand you're learning to code," Elizabeth said as they stepped onto the trail.

Sutton didn't want to brag. But learning to code made it sound like she was still learning how to read binary. "I'm programming my robot for obstacle avoidance right now."

"Wow!" Elizabeth said.

Luis ducked a flying insect. "In *The Book Scav-*

enger, Emily and James pass coded messages to each other in a bucket between their bedrooms."

"That's not coding," Sutton said.

"Well, sure it is," said her dad. "Just a different kind." He winked at Luis, but Luis didn't see. Luis's eyes were busy pinging back and forth, watching out for peanuts or gluten or stray shellfish in the forest.

"I research diabetes," said Elizabeth. "No coding involved. But I know we couldn't complete our current trial without SQL to mine the data. That's related to coding, right?"

Sutton didn't know what that was. She wanted to look it up on her favorite science website. But her dad still had her tablet.

"Whoa!" Luis stopped suddenly in front of an especially enormous tree. "Check that out! It looks like the World Tree from *The Sword of Summer*!"

Sutton's dad strolled up behind Luis and admired the tree's twisty roots. "Ah yes, Norse mythology, right? Each of those folds in the tree might just lead to one of the nine worlds!"

"The world of elves!" Luis said.

"The world of dwarves," Martin added.

"The world of frost giants!" Luis reached his arms up to make himself look as giant as possible.

Sutton scowled. So Elizabeth was a scientist. And Luis and her dad both liked books. But that didn't mean everyone was automatically going to be the best of friends.

Luis didn't seem to have any problem with getting to know Sutton's dad, though. He asked questions about being in the symphony. He mimed playing the saxophone. He seemed to have forgotten to be worried about surprise shellfish in the woods.

"How did you find out Luis is allergic to bees?" she asked.

Elizabeth shuddered. "That was a terrible day. He was in first grade, and when I got a call at work from the school office, I was sure he'd been exposed to peanuts at lunch. We learned about most of his food allergies when he was much younger."

"Around two hundred people die each year because of food allergies." Sutton immediately wished she could take that back. It was probably a terrible thing to say to a mom whose kid had food allergies.

Elizabeth nodded. "Yes, and peanuts are one of the biggest culprits. But when the school called, it was because he'd been picking daisies during recess and gotten stung! Thankfully, the school nurse knew what to do."

Sutton knew too. When she'd gotten stuck with her bot the night before, she'd taken a break and looked up bee-sting allergies and peanut allergies. She wanted to be prepared.

What she didn't look up was basic first aid, which might have come in handy. Because right then, Luis tripped over a root and fell, face-first, onto the trail.

CHAPTER TWENTY

Luis

Luis scrambled up, hoping no one had noticed his fall. He'd been distracted by a cool tunnel up ahead. Maybe everyone else had been distracted too. Though no one else would have recognized it as exactly like the tunnel on the Whitlow School's grounds that was really an undiscovered portal into the headquarters of the Dark Force.

"Luis!"

No such luck. Martin was right there, and more footsteps slapped the trail behind him. "Oh, love!" his mom cried out as she caught up.

"I'm okay." He'd only tripped. True, his forehead throbbed a little where he'd smacked the ground. And his knees were definitely skinned. He might've landed funny on his elbow, too.

Sutton stood apart from the others. "I have a first aid kit," she said.

Luis had a first aid kit in his backpack too. So that was something they had in common—they both liked to be prepared.

"I'm okay!" He stood up and ignored the sting in his knees, moving past his mom so she wouldn't look too closely at his scrapes. "Look over there!"

The parents kept hovering, but Sutton looked where he was pointing—at a narrow opening in a dense thicket of bushes up ahead.

"It looks like a secret passageway," he said.

"Like it might lead to Narnia!" Martin added.

Luis wasn't going to point out that if it were going to lead to Narnia, it would be inside an English professor's country manor, and it would be a wardrobe, not a tunnel. Martin was playing along and the focus had shifted off Luis's fall, so the details of classic fantasy novels weren't really the main point right now.

"Yeah, like a portal! Let's check it out."

The girls hung back, but Martin joined Luis,

ready to go have tea with a faun in the land of eternal winter. Unfortunately, Martin was thwarted by the fact that the tunnel was far too small for an adult.

"Oh man, I don't fit," he said. "But you do!"

Luis looked at the tunnel. He didn't especially want to go in there by himself. Going through a portal to have an adventure with a traveling companion was one thing; going through a portal to fend for oneself in a foreign, magical land was totally different.

"Sutton," Martin called. "Come here! Check this out."

"She doesn't have to—"

Martin clapped his hands and the sound bounced off the trees around them. "Oh! Or you know what else it's like? *Alice in Wonderland*!"

That portal was at least outside, but it was more of a hole in the ground that Alice fell down. And it would probably not be the best way to get Sutton on board. She had already made clear what she thought of fantasy stories at the MoPOP. Luis decided he'd appeal to her scientist side instead.

"Maybe there's a new species of plant to discover in there!"

"Discovery Park has existed since 1973," Sutton

said. "I'm pretty sure all the discoveries have been made."

Luis was trying, even after Sutton had been so standoffish the last time they were together. But here she was, doing it again. Luis's chest started to feel tight.

Martin frowned. "Sutton . . . "

"I know," she said. "Keep an open mind."

She said it like she'd heard it a million times but wasn't convinced. (What kind of scientist made any discoveries without an open mind?) How mad had she been about coming if her dad had to tell her to keep an open mind over and over again? Luis didn't really want an adventure partner who'd been forced to go along. But he didn't want to go into the tunnel alone, either.

It wasn't that he truly thought there was anything beastly lying in wait. But he had enough of an imagination to know it was a possibility.

"Here's my hypothesis," Sutton said. "This portal leads to a world where the kids have scratches, bug bites, and no way out"—she held up a hand to shush her dad's objections—"but I like experiments."

And she marched toward the portal.

"Wait!" Luis called, scrambling to catch up.

"Careful, Luis!" his mom called behind him.

"See you on the other side!" called Martin. "It looks like it lets out right around the bend."

Luis caught up with Sutton at the entrance. "Can I go first?" he said. "It was my idea."

"Sure," Sutton said. "You do know it's not really a portal to another world, right?"

Luis considered what he knew about science. Scientists like his mom made hypotheses, which was a big word for guesses. Then they gathered facts and did experiments to see if their guesses were right. They were really, really big on proof.

"Can you prove it's *not* a portal to another world?" he asked.

Sutton opened her mouth to snap back a smart answer—not smart in the way they both knew she was, but smart in the way their parents always told them not to be. But no words came.

Luis didn't wait for an answer. He started through the tunnel, pushing branches aside and holding them so they wouldn't snap back and whomp Sutton in the face. Though if he was honest with himself, the idea of whomping Sutton in the face was not unsatisfactory.

"So what kind of science do you like?" he said. There had to be something they could talk about.

"All kinds. I won the Pacific Northwest Science

Fair at the seventh grade level. When I was in third grade. Ow!"

Oops. He'd let one of the branches go too quickly. "Sorry. Wow, cool. What's your favorite part about science?"

"The facts."

This was a fact: Luis had thought the tunnel was a few feet long. The bushes hadn't seemed that deep. But now he couldn't see where it would end, and the branches poked and prodded on every side.

When Sutton bumped into him, they poked and prodded even deeper.

"Why'd you stop?" she said.

"Sorry." Luis moved forward. But it was no use. Straight ahead, the tunnel ended with no opening. They would have to turn back. He tried to turn to face Sutton, who would have to lead the way back out. But a bramble caught the back of his shirt and dug into his skin whenever he tried to turn.

Sutton had been right. They shouldn't have come into the tunnel. Luis was surrounded on all sides by branches. Some bees nested in trees or bushes. If something stung him in the middle of all these brambles, he wouldn't be able to reach his EpiPen. Or his mom!

"Hey, are you okay?"

Luis was breathing fast. Too fast. "It dead-ends," he gasped. "We're stuck!"

"Hey!" Sutton grabbed his shoulder. "That's a dumb way to breathe. The oxygen can't get to your lungs like that. Breathe with me."

She started breathing slow, noisy breaths. She sounded like Luis's mom doing yoga. Luis pretended she *was* Mom doing yoga. He took a breath with her, and then another.

"Luis," she said, her hand still gripping his shoulder. "It looks like a dead end. But it's not. It turns. I can't get around you. So you're going to have to keep walking."

Luis's breath was almost back to normal. "It turns?"

"Well. It might."

"It's not a fact?"

"I guess it's a hypothesis we have to test."

"Okay." Luis took another breath. "The thing is, there's something caught on my shirt?"

"Hang on." Sutton worked some magic (or, from her perspective, did something with a logical cause and effect) and freed Luis from the bramble that had him trapped. "Try now."

Luis took a step. Then another step. He was free.

And it was tight, but Sutton kept her hand on his shoulder. They tested the hypothesis. Sutton kept doing long, slow yoga breaths. Luis followed her breaths, while Sutton followed his steps.

When they reached the dead end, Luis gasped again—but this time in relief. Sutton's hypothesis had been correct. It had been impossible to see before, but the tunnel turned. In a few more feet, they'd be out in the open.

"You were right!" Luis said. Where the tunnel ended, there was almost room for them to switch positions. "Do you want to go first now?"

"Nope," Sutton said. "You can do it."

She was right. Nothing had stung him. His fingers and toes weren't numb. Luis made the turn and headed for the clearing. He wasn't even thinking about magical lands anymore. He was too focused on getting out.

His shirt snagged on a branch again, just as he was about to exit the tunnel. Sutton reached around and snapped it free before he even had to ask. And then Luis was out, Sutton right behind him.

Their parents were nowhere to be seen.

CHAPTER TWENTY-ONE

Sutton

Sutton dropped her backpack. She would never admit it to her dad—even if he'd been standing where the tunnel let out like he said he would—but her shoulders were already starting to ache. She looked around the clearing.

Their parents should have gotten here already. They would have moved more quickly along the main trail, with their longer legs and no poky branches getting in their way. So where were they?

"Mom!" Luis called out.

Sutton squatted down and unzipped her pack. "Want a snack while we wait?"

"Where are they?" Luis asked. The clearing was about the size of the basketball court where the regional robotics competition was held. It was surrounded by thick woods on all sides. "Which way did we come from?"

That was easy. The tunnel was right behind them. "They'll get here." Sutton examined Luis's face. It looked normal—a warm brown, several shades darker than his mom's. But his breathing was still a little funny. "I think you should have something to eat."

Sutton had been very careful not to pack any snacks with Luis's allergens.

But Luis returned to the tunnel entrance and peered inside—as though their parents could fit through there when the kids had barely made it. Then he walked back and forth along the bushes, trying to find where their parents might come through to meet them.

He reminded her of the mini-bot, spinning in circles, unable to find the next turn in the maze. Unlike the bot, which would keep trying until its charge ran out, Luis finally gave up and came to sit next to Sutton, who had spread a towel on the bug-infested ground before sitting.

She bit into an apple. If she closed her eyes, she could imagine she was sitting on the floor of her room. She did have *some* imagination after all. Except birds kept chirping. Something buzzed past her ear. And her fingers were itching for a screen to swipe.

People, not pixels.

But she didn't have people! She only had Luis. Her dad and even Elizabeth would make it people. Sutton took another bite of apple. If her dad hadn't shown up by the time she finished the apple, then she might start to worry. A little. It was a big apple. There was time.

It was quiet for a minute, except for the birds and bugs and Sutton's chewing. Then Luis said, "I think we have to work together if we're going to defeat the Dark Force."

Sutton paused, midbite. "I have no idea what that means."

"It's from a book. There are these two schools for magical misfits, and normally they're clashing and in competition, but then the Dark Force starts trying to defeat them by taking control of the students at the rival magical academy."

Sutton blinked at him. She really did not get this kid. But she had promised to try. "What's the book called?"

"Oh, you wouldn't be interested."

She frowned. "I could be. But also my friend Sabina is really into fantasy, and she has a birthday at the end of the summer."

"Oh!" Luis brightened. "I could give you a bunch of suggestions! Has she read *The Serpent's Secret*? Or *Shadows of Sherwood*? Or *The Jumbies*?"

"I don't know. What was the one you were just describing?"

Luis's cheeks went pink. "Oh. She can't read that."

"Why not?"

"Because it's not a real book! It's just a story I'm writing."

"Oh." That was pretty neat, actually. Sutton might not have enjoyed reading stories, but she had a full and complete appreciation for how difficult it was to create them. Her dad made her do a creative-writing unit every year. "So what does your story have to do with our situation?"

"I was saying our parents aren't coming," Luis said. "It's only the two of us now, and even if we don't see things the same way, we have to work together. We can't sit here doing nothing. If they were coming, they'd be here by now."

Sutton frowned and took the last bite of her apple. Logic said they should stay in one place and their parents would come. But logic didn't always work. Sure, it could be relied on most of the time, but there were outliers. Maybe some creative thinking was exactly what she needed to get her bot through its maze. And maybe if she tried things Luis's way, she would learn something about how to do that.

"Okay." She got to her feet and dusted herself off.

"Wait, really?"

She shrugged and started walking around the edges of the clearing. "There has to be a way out somewhere. Do you know how many people hike in Discovery Park every year?"

"But adults don't fit through that tunnel."

"I'm sure we're not the first kids in this situation."

Upon reflection, they probably were the first kids in this particular situation: on a second family date after the first rather disastrous one, mismatched in every way except one—they were both completely unprepared to survive alone in the wilderness.

"Is your mom outdoorsy?" Sutton asked as she

prodded a particularly thorny-looking bush.

Luis paused. "She wasn't, before your dad."

"Yeah, my dad was never into hiking before he met your mom."

"Oh." He was quiet for a minute, except for a tiny yelp Sutton thought might have been caused by a ladybug flitting past. "Actually, she used to do outdoorsy stuff with my dad. They got married on a beach. And climbed a volcano in Guatemala. But that was a long time ago."

Sutton realized she hadn't asked her dad about Luis's parents. Were they divorced? Was his dad around? Something about the wistfulness in his voice right then made her think maybe he wasn't.

On her second time around the clearing, Sutton saw something she hadn't noticed before. Tucked behind an overgrown bush, there was a trail. It wasn't a tiny, narrow passage like the tunnel. It was an actual trail.

"There is a way out!" she announced. "A trail behind this tree!"

"Really?"

"We can stand up and everything!"

Luis cheered, grabbed his backpack, and headed for the trail.

"Wait." Sutton grabbed Luis's arm. "Are we sure this is the best idea? My dad would tell me to wait here."

"But 'stay where you are' is for when you're lost and your parents can come find you. They can't get through the tunnel! Plus, what if they're much farther down the trail?" Luis said. "What if, from the outside, it looks like the tunnel goes on a longer way? They would keep walking. But by now they're probably worried too. My mom is probably freaking out!"

His breath started to come in short bursts again.

Sutton wasn't going on a quest. This wasn't a magical land and there was no sinister force trying to curse them. But Luis had a point. Her dad was probably freaking out too. "Okay." Sutton slung her backpack onto her shoulders. "Let's check it out."

It didn't take them long to reach the end of the path. Where the trail divided into three more paths. Sutton groaned.

"Three paths!" Luis's breathing was back to normal. "Three's an important number in classic fairy tales. Three bears, three wise men, three billy goats gruff . . ."

Sutton waited. Then she watched his face fall. Now they were on the same page. Having three different options wasn't actually a good thing.

"Okay, we can't panic," he said. "Whenever characters in books get lost, panicking just takes up time."

Sutton was very proud of herself for not rolling her eyes. He was the one who kept panicking.

"We should build a cairn," he blurted.

"A what?"

"A cairn. Explorers use them to mark their paths. If we take one path and end up back here, we'll know which path we already tried."

Sutton fiddled with the end of her backpack strap. Sometimes Luis's ideas were wacko. But sometimes they were so wacko, they ended up being good.

"In *Kaya's Escape*, she builds a cairn on the Buffalo Trail and it helps her people find her!"

Sutton didn't know who Kaya was, but she vaguely remembered cairns from a history lesson. "We have to decide which path we're taking before we build the cairn, right?"

"Yeah, I guess? I mean, yeah! Where do you think we should go?"

Deciding which way to go had not been Sutton's greatest strength lately, at least if she considered herself the brains of the bot. Which she did. "If my dad hadn't taken my tablet, this would be a lot easier. But I remember from the maps that the park entrance was to the north."

Luis looked one way, and then another. "So . . . which way's north?"

Sutton peered at the sky. The sun hadn't risen up above the trees yet. (She was kind of glad, because while she knew she was supposed to be able to figure out directions from the position of the sun, she didn't really know how.)

"If only I hadn't taken off my watch with GPS," she said. "Even a compass would help. . . ."

"Oh! I have a compass!"

Sutton stared at Luis. Why hadn't he said so sooner?

He set his pack down, rummaged around, and came up with a compass. He handed it to her. "I don't know how to use it."

"Then why do you have it?"

He shrugged. "Because that's what explorers have." Then quieter: "And it belonged to my dad."

It *belonged* to his dad. Past tense.

"I'm really sorry. Is it . . . the only thing of his you have?"

Luis reached like he might grab the compass back, but then held off. "No. We have lots of stuff and pictures. Even videos. But it still matters to me!"

Of course it mattered to him. Sutton's mom was alive; she was just on the other side of the globe. She was like a mother penguin who'd left her egg to be cared for by its father, not because she didn't care about it, but because that was what worked for their family. The mother penguin had to return to the sea to feed, after all the effort of laying an egg. Sutton's mom had to return to the research station to do the work she was meant to do. Important work, work that could save whole ecosystems. And Sutton still missed her all the time.

"Well, your dad's compass is going to get us out of here," she said. "So I'm glad he left it to you."

Sutton knew how to use a compass, even though they were ancient technology. Her dad always made her learn the principles behind a technology before she used it, like how to do the math herself before she used a calculator.

She found north with the compass and then

decided which of the three trails would take them north. Sort of.

"Cool! So we put a cairn here to mark which way we went. That way, if we try to retrace our steps, or someone comes through here looking for us—"

"Does it matter what size rocks?" Sutton asked, handing the compass back to Luis. She hoisted the biggest rock she saw and lugged it toward the trail-head.

Luis shrugged. "It's just a pile of rocks. Whatever we can find." He started gathering more rocks.

"But if we want it to be stable, we should think about it like engineers," Sutton pointed out. "A random pile will get knocked over by any animal that walks past."

Luis froze. "Are there animals out here?"

Of course there were animals. It was a forest. But hopefully nothing more menacing than squirrels. Not bears. Or wildcats. What else lived in the wilderness of the Pacific Northwest? Sutton's mind flashed to news reports about mountain lions along hiking trails.

But Discovery Park was in the middle of a major city. There couldn't be mountain lions. Could there?

Sutton shoved the biggest rock into the center of the trail entrance. "We need a stable base," she said, "as wide as possible."

Working together, it didn't take long before the cairn was built and they were on their way.

CHAPTER TWENTY-TWO

Luis

The next time they came to a fork in the trail, Sutton offered to show Luis how to use the compass. It was his, after all. On the one hand, after getting separated today, his mother would probably never allow him to go outside ever again. But on the other hand, all the old-timey adventurers in his favorite books knew how to use a compass. It seemed like a useful skill.

Luis held the compass in his palm. His papi's compass. A little arrow on the compass pointed to the *N*, which Luis knew stood for north. "That way!"

he said. Which was weird, because it was back the way they had come.

"No." Sutton grabbed the compass, but then she held it out for Luis to see. "That arrow never moves. Here. If I look at the red arrow, it seems like that way is north!" She turned another direction. "Now that way is north!" She turned another direction. "Now that way is north!"

Luis frowned. "Is it broken?"

"No. You have to line up the red arrow that always points at the N with the floating arrow that spins. When they line up, it's pointing north." She handed the compass back to Luis.

He turned it slowly, carefully until the arrows lined up. "So . . . that way?"

"Right," Sutton said.

Luis swelled with accomplishment as he wrapped his hands around his papi's compass. Luis didn't really remember him, but from his mom's pictures, Papi had loved the outdoors. He hiked and mountain biked and rock climbed. He used to run marathons back in Guatemala. Maybe his mom had been missing the outdoors all these years, stuck inside with Luis so he wouldn't get stung by a bee.

"Thanks for showing me," Luis said.

Sutton smiled. It might have been the first time Luis had seen her smile. "The next time I see you, I'll show you how to use GPS," she promised. "It's much cooler."

Luis grinned. When they'd first met, Sutton hadn't seemed interested in a next time. This was progress. Of course, he hoped next time wouldn't involve the possibility of getting lost in the woods. Maybe Sutton and her dad could come over to their house. They could make an allergen-free meal, and Luis could show Sutton his Penelope Bell notebook. Maybe.

"Do you think there'll be a next time?" he asked.

"As long as we don't die from exposure," she said.

Luis froze and Sutton burst out laughing. "I'm joking," she added. "There are plenty of things we could die from out here. It's way too warm to die from exposure, though. I'm pretty sure that means, like, freezing to death."

This was not making Luis feel any better.

"And," she said, more serious this time, "there'll probably be a next time."

They came to another fork, or at least it looked like a fork. Except the path that continued north only went a few feet before it dead-ended in blackberry brambles. The other option was to take the path that turned left, which sent them directly west.

"This isn't right," Luis said.

"No," Sutton agreed. "But on the bright side, we can't go very far west before we'll reach the water."

Was that a bright side? "We don't want to go west at all! The parking lot is north! My mom said if we got separated, to meet in the parking lot."

"So we go west until the next chance to go north. Maybe it's not the most direct way, but it'll still get us there."

She set off to the west. Luis followed, mostly because he wasn't going to be left behind. After a few minutes, Sutton spoke up again. "I'm programming this robot to go through a maze," she said.

"Okay."

"It's not a big robot like at the MoPOP with all sorts of buttons and abilities. It's just a little mini-bot."

"It still sounds cool."

"Thanks. Anyway, I've been trying to program it to get through a maze by the quickest route possible. I'm doing something wrong in the code that I can't figure out."

Luis had no idea how to help with robots, but he

wanted to keep Sutton talking. "Could you ask your mom? Isn't she some kind of scientist?"

"She's a biologist. She doesn't know a lot about coding, but she does think sort of like I do. So maybe. I don't know when she'll get back in town, though. Anyway, I was thinking about how my focus has been on getting the bot through the maze as quickly as possible, right? That's the goal I set when I started."

"Maybe the bot will still get through by a different route?"

"Exactly! And maybe speed isn't the most important thing."

"Yeah!" Luis thought about Penelope Bell and her friends, rushing to get to Alistair Academy before the Dark Force took over the school. If they hadn't been so focused on getting there quickly, they could have gathered more misfits to their side for the battle ahead. "Though I definitely would rather get to the parking lot before dark."

CHAPTER TWENTY-THREE

Sutton

Sutton had been right about the water.

Eventually the westbound trail brought them to a clearing that overlooked Puget Sound, a huge expanse of water between Seattle and the Olympic Mountain range. Between Seattle and the mountains, though, lay a string of islands where Sutton's mom used to take her on day trips.

Since Sutton had been five when her parents got divorced, she only remembered snapshots from that time. Moving from the house they all shared in Ballard to the apartment building in South Lake

Union. Missing her mom at bedtime. Meeting Mrs. Banerjee and Moti, who was a brand-new puppy.

On weekends, Sutton's mom would take her on special outings. They'd go to the Science Center or the Children's Museum or the Seattle Aquarium. Sometimes they'd take a ferry across to one of the islands and get ice cream that wasn't really any different than ice cream they could get in Seattle, but it was special because it was with her mom.

But then one weekend they took a ferry out to Whidbey Island, and Sutton was licking a huge scoop of blackberry-honey ice cream when her mom explained about a new job. A new job that would send her far away for long stretches of time. Important work! Female scientists! Saving penguins!

They hadn't gone back to the islands again.

"Are you okay?" Luis asked.

Sutton nodded and turned away from the view of the water and the mountains. And the islands. "Yep," she said. "So if the water is west, that way is north."

There was a clear, well-traveled trail heading north. "Yes!" Luis did a little leap on his way toward the path. He was so busy dancing around, he nearly crashed into a grizzled old man with an intricately carved walking stick. "Oh!"

The man looked from Luis to Sutton, and then he continued on the path.

"Wait!" Luis called out. "We're trying to reach the north parking lot?"

The man stopped. "Yes?"

"Are we on the right path?"

"That depends," the man said, "on how you want to travel."

Sutton glanced at Luis. His eyes were huge, like he'd just met Dumbledore in the flesh. Even though this guy was obviously a quirky local, like the lady at the farmers' market who spun dog fur into yarn and sold scarves and mittens, even Sutton had to admit the man could have leapt off the pages of one of Luis's stories. And maybe this would all be just a little more fun if she pretended he had.

"Flying would be nice," she said. "If that's an option."

Luis's eyebrows shot up, but the old man didn't bat an eye. He just turned and looked out over the water. "Inadvisable," he finally said. "Given current wind conditions, I fear you'd be blown straight out to sea."

"We want to get to the north parking lot," Luis said. "As quickly as possible."

"Ah. Well then, I would not advise you stay on this path. It is quite roundabout, twisting and turning for more than two miles. However, you can always take the Fort Buford Trail for about a quarter mile. It switches back a few times, but stay on it. You'll reach a stream with a little bridge, and once you cross the bridge you'll be able to see the main trail. That'll take you to the parking lot."

He reached into his back pocket and pulled out a map folded over so many times the writing had faded in the creases. "This will get you from the trail to the parking lot."

"Won't you need it?" Luis asked.

The man smiled and stared out at the water. "No," he said. "I won't need it."

Then he carried on along the path, thumping his walking stick with each step.

"Thank you!" Luis called out as Sutton examined the map. Then he turned to her. "Flying?"

She shrugged. "I half expected it to work. He might have cast a spell and zapped us straight into the parking lot, but I guess this map is good enough." She found a clearing right next to Puget Sound, which had to be where they stood. "Fort Buford Trail . . ."

"Are you sure we should go that way?" Luis said. "It sounds complicated. We could get lost again. Weren't you saying that maybe the fastest way isn't always the best?"

Sutton considered this. It had been true when she was thinking about her bot. "Yeah, but also I'm going to need a bathroom soon."

The Fort Buford trail was easy to find. There was even a signpost. But it went uphill in a totally ridiculous way—up toward the right for a while, and then over to the left, and then to the right again.

"Do you know how far a quarter of a mile is?" Luis asked.

"One thousand three hundred and twenty feet."

Luis gaped at her. "How did you know that?"

"It's math." Sutton knew the math answer. But she had no idea what it felt like to walk a quarter of a mile. "I think we should be almost there."

"There!" Luis called out.

Sure enough, there was a stream. If she were more adventurous, she could probably hop over it in one leap. But thankfully, a sturdy wooden footbridge stretched across the stream. Bridges often made Sutton nervous. She hated driving across Lake Washington on the 520—a bridge that actually floated on the water. The footbridge over the stream was close to the water, but she could see the sturdy posts that would support her weight. Plus, she'd be across it in about three steps.

"We're almost there," Luis sang out, hurrying toward the bridge.

"We're almost to the trail." Sutton pulled the map out of her pocket. "Let me see how far it will be after that."

She unfolded the map and found the bridge. She kept a finger there and with her other hand found the north parking lot. She traced the distance between the two points, then consulted the key on the map.

"Come on, Sutton!" Luis called from the bridge.

Sutton looked up. One moment Luis was waving happily. The next moment he was screaming and windmilling his arms. Sutton dropped the map and ran.

"What's wrong?"

"Bee!" he screamed. "Bee!"

With all of Luis's flailing, it took Sutton a minute to even see the bee.

But she would be flailing too if a bee sting could send her into anaphylactic shock. They would need an ambulance, and Sutton had no way to call one. But they wouldn't need an ambulance if she could get to the bee before the bee got to Luis.

Sutton reached Luis on the other side of the bridge, where he was still in constant motion. The bee darted around him. Sutton looked for something to use to swat it away. Hitting a bee with a stick required more athletic precision than Sutton would ever have in her life. Plus, she might smash Luis while she was at it. He'd probably rather be smashed in the head with a stick than stung by a bee. But still. There had to be another way.

"Can you stop waving your arms?" Sutton called. If she could get a clear shot at the bee . . .

"It'll get me if I'm still!" Luis yelped.

"Not if you trust me! Imagine one of your stories! There are . . . lasers all around you, and if you hit one the alarm will go off and . . . wake the ogre!"

Luis stilled.

"Crouch down in a ball," Sutton said. She knew what she had to do, and she was ready to do it. Luis had been afraid to see her again. After all the mis-communication at the MoPOP, she couldn't blame him. But she could show him that wasn't who she was. She needed to get Luis out of the way. And she needed the bee to hover where she could reach it, instead of above Luis's head.

Luis crouched. The bee buzzed down lower.

With the hand-eye coordination of a seasoned video-game player, Sutton's hands shot out and trapped the bee between her palms. "Got it."

Luis jerked his head up. "You killed it?"

"Not exactly."

His eyes bounced to her cupped hands. He gasped in horror as she gasped in pain.

She opened her hands and the bee flew out. The stinger was stuck in the center of Sutton's right palm. "He'll die now," she said. "They can't live without a stinger, you know."

Luis nodded gravely. "I can't believe you did that for me."

Sutton shrugged, though her palm really hurt. "This family date would have been even worse than the MoPOP if you'd died."

"I have tweezers in here somewhere. We have to remove the stinger."

Sutton looked at her palm. The sight of the stinger jutting out made her a little woozy.

"Here, sit down," Luis said, guiding her to a large rock. He fumbled around in his pack and came out with his first aid kit.

"That's the same one I have!" Sutton said.

Luis grinned and reached for her hand, but Sutton snatched it back.

"Wait," she said. "Are you sure you should touch it? There might still be venom on it."

"That's what the tweezers are for." Luis pulled her hand back, and before she could protest again, the stinger was out. Once a bandage had been applied, Luis pulled Sutton to her feet. "Are you okay to walk now?"

"I'm okay. Let's get back to the parking lot." She felt a little embarrassed, but she didn't know why. "Hey, Luis? Thanks."

"You took a bee sting for me," he said. "We're like soldiers on the battlefield together. I wasn't going to leave you behind."

Sutton reached for the trail map to double-check the way to the parking lot, which was when she realized she'd dropped it on the other side of the stream. "Hang on." She stepped onto the footbridge to retrieve the map, but as she did, something flitted past her face—another bee?—and she jerked her head around. As she spun, she lost her balance. It all happened far too quickly to understand what was going on.

Sutton heard a shout—had she shouted, or was it Luis? And then he was there, grabbing onto her arm, and then they were both falling.

CHAPTER TWENTY-FOUR

Luis

It wasn't so much a fall as a topple, and Luis hit the water only seconds after he grabbed onto Sutton. To be more precise, his rear end plopped through a couple of inches of water onto the muddy bottom of the stream.

Looking back, he probably shouldn't have grabbed onto Sutton as he fell. He had meant to stop her from falling. He might have pulled her in instead.

When she popped up, gasping, he thought she might yell at him. He definitely did not expect her to yell, "There's another bee!"

The stream truly was only a stream—the water didn't even come up to Luis's knees when he jumped to his feet. "Where? I don't see it!"

"There! Oh . . . wait."

Luis followed Sutton's outstretched finger to an orange butterfly flitting around the bridge. He looked to Sutton. She looked at him.

"I'm not allergic to butterflies," he said.

She snorted, then threw a hand over her face to hold in any amusement. But then Luis let out a snort of his own, and they both dissolved into giggles.

Luis sat back down in the stream. He was soaked already anyway. "On the bright side," he said, "our parents will probably never make us go on a hike again."

Sutton giggled harder.

Luis stopped giggling, however, when he saw something else flying through the air. It wasn't a bug of any sort. It wasn't something he was allergic to. It was the map. And it had been lifted by a gust of wind to dance over the water.

"The map!" Luis and Sutton both cried at the same time. They lunged to reach it; they never had a chance. It took a dive and landed on the surface of the water.

Luis splashed through the stream to reach the map, but when he got there, it was already dissolving. He held up the sopping, gloppy remains of the paper.

Sutton gave a grim nod. "Well, no more map," she said. She stood up and waded out of the stream. "But look over there—that must be the main trail. Once we're on it, maybe we'll run into other hikers."

Luis was imagining they'd never be found. They'd have to climb trees to sleep in for the night, so creatures on the ground wouldn't get them.

Sutton hoisted her pack onto her shoulders and headed for the trail. Luis scrambled out of the water. After everything they had been through, he wasn't going to be separated from Sutton now! His shoes squished as he ran to catch up. Sutton walked on ahead, looking like an experienced hiker. Except that she was dripping all over the trail.

She had suffered a bee sting for him. He and Sutton had gotten off to a terrible start, and she didn't seem like someone he had much in common with. But maybe that didn't matter. She had acted like a friend today.

He caught up with her. Her shoes were squishing too.

"My mom's been really happy since she met your dad," he said.

Sutton grunted and shifted her backpack.

"I'm not saying it's not weird," he added. "It's totally weird."

"How long have you guys been . . . just you guys?"

"My mom and I? As long as I remember. My dad died when I was two." Before she had to ask, Luis added, "Cancer."

"I'm sorry."

"She hasn't dated anyone since. So this is a big deal. Not only going out with your dad, but wanting me to meet him. Wanting us to meet."

Sutton was quiet for a minute, and Luis wondered if he'd said too much. Then she said, "My dad has gone on a few dates since my parents divorced. But never more than two or three with the same person. I've never met someone he's dating before. In fact, the night you got bitten by the guinea pig—"

"I didn't get bitten—"

"I thought he was going to propose."

Luis stumbled and only stayed upright because Sutton grabbed his backpack. He liked Martin. And he and Sutton were starting to get along. He'd thought about his mom getting remarried someday, sure. Hearing it out loud, said by another person, was something else entirely.

"Are you okay? I could be wrong," Sutton added. "It's just a hunch. He didn't show me a ring or anything."

Luis's mom wore her wedding ring on a chain around her neck. What would happen to it if she had a ring from Martin? What about all the pictures of Papi around the house? And his art?

"Honestly," Sutton continued, "there's not a lot of evidence for my hypothesis. Just all the dates. And how happy he seems. Mostly the way they keep trying to get us together."

"To see how we work as a family?"

"Maybe." Sutton kicked a rock. "Or maybe they just want us to be friends. My dad's always trying to get me to make more friends."

"Don't you want friends?"

"I have friends. I just don't need a whole orchestra-full like he does. There are kids on my robotics team and in our homeschool group. Kids in my building, even. We live in an apartment."

Luis had been so focused on the novelty of his mom dating that it hadn't even occurred to him that there could be more changes ahead. If their parents got married, where would they live? He loved their house on Queen Anne. But it wasn't big enough for two more people. Maybe they would be expected to move into the downtown apartment?

Would Martin try to act like his dad? What on earth would it be like to live with Sutton? They had made progress so far today, but not that much progress.

"What if he planned to propose today?" Luis said. "While we were all together? That spot overlooking the water would have been perfect."

"Well, I guess we ruined that!" Sutton laughed. "I don't think so, though. I think he would talk to me before a step like that."

"It's the biggest step," Luis said.

"Yeah. Hey, look, people!" Sutton said, interrupting his spiraling thoughts. "We must be close!"

Coming around a bend up ahead was a couple walking a black Lab.

"Dog!" Luis yelped.

"Are you allergic to dogs, too?"

"No, they just scare me."

"Do you want to pet him?" the woman called.

"Sure." Sutton jogged over.

"Bella's really friendly," the woman called to Luis, who had plastered himself against a tree.

"He's allergic," Sutton said. And he was, only not to dogs. "We're trying to reach the north parking lot. Are we headed in the right direction?"

"Yep." The man pointed back the way they'd come from. "Right around that bend, the trail splits. Head right, and just after you pass between two big boulders, you'll see a bridge. Cross the bridge and the parking lot is right through the trees!" He paused. "Are you kids here with your parents, or . . . ?"

"We got separated," Sutton said. "We're okay now, though. Come on, Luis!"

Luis stuck as close as possible to the trees as he moved along the path past the black Lab. "Bella" meant beautiful in Spanish, but beauty was in the eye of the beholder.

He scooted past them and met Sutton where the trail split. "The two boulders!" he said, pointing. They were close now.

They raced together, four shoes squishing, so excited to finally reach the parking lot. Like the man had said, there was a bridge right beyond the boulders.

It wasn't a sturdy wooden bridge, like the one over the stream. This was a rope bridge that stretched across a deep ravine. "Cool!" Luis cried as he bounced onto the bridge.

CHAPTER TWENTY-FIVE

Sutton

Sutton froze between the two boulders.

She watched the bridge swing wildly as Luis jumped onto it.

He turned back. "What are you waiting for? Let's go!"

Sutton was not going to cross that bridge. That bridge did not obey any of the laws of engineering. It was made of ropes! Ropes that would shake when she stepped on them. Ropes that could snap at any second!

"Come on, we're almost there!"

Sutton backed up farther. She was safe between the two boulders.

Luis hopped off the bridge and bounded over.

"Are you afraid of heights?"

"No."

Luis looked from Sutton back to the bridge.

"I'm afraid," Sutton said, "of super-dangerous bridges!"

Luis looked thoughtful for a minute. Sutton expected him to try to convince her that the bridge was safe. That was what her dad would do. And it wouldn't work.

But instead, Luis said, "Yeah. It's *super* dangerous. But the thing is, the dragon that lives in the ravine is asleep. So now's the perfect time to cross."

Sutton frowned. She was so busy trying to figure out how to respond, she let Luis pull her over to where the bridge began.

"See?" he said, looking over the edge. "He's zonked out. But he won't be for long. And when he wakes up? Yikes. One puff and the whole bridge goes up in smoke."

He stepped onto the bridge. It shook like crazy.

Sutton wanted to run back to the boulders. But Luis was holding out his hand.

"We have to go now, Sutton. The dragon will wake up soon. And we have to warn the people on the other side."

If Sutton thought for a second about what was real, she would never be brave enough to step onto this bridge. But if she tried it Luis's way, if only for a minute . . .

"What if . . ." This was so weird, but if anyone would get it, Luis would. "What if it's not a dragon? What if we're penguins, and the ravine is filled with hungry sea lions? But we have to cross to get to the sea or we'll never be able to feed our chicks?"

Luis blinked at her. For one horrifying second, Sutton thought he might laugh at her. Then he nodded. "Sea lions are terrifying," he said. "And penguin chicks are the cutest thing in the world! We have to save them."

She stepped onto the bridge. It swung and her heart galloped in her chest, but Luis gripped her hand.

"Hurry," he said. "I just heard a sea lion roar!"

He raced along the bridge. Sutton took a deep breath and then raced after him. Partly because she didn't want to be left behind. And partly because they had to escape the sea lions.

When she reached the other side, Luis cheered. He gave her a high five as she jumped off the bridge.

"We did it!" he cried. "We saved the penguin chicks!"

"Thank you, Luis," Sutton said, trying to catch her breath.

He shrugged. "I didn't do anything. Come on." He grabbed her hand again and pulled her toward the trees.

Sutton had completely forgotten the throbbing pain of the bee sting on her palm, the squelch of her soaked shoes, even the terrifying passage over the bridge they had crossed. The only thing that mattered now was seeing her dad.

When they burst through the trees and into the parking lot, she didn't see him. Instead, Sutton saw a whole circle of adults crowded around the faded map. A group planning their hike, she thought at first. But there were park rangers and police officers too. One of the police officers was giving instructions.

"So one group will head toward the rope bridge," the officer said, his gaze down on a clipboard and his finger pointing directly at Sutton and Luis.

Someone turned to see where she was pointing and then said, "Wait, is that them?"

As one, the group swiveled to look at Sutton and Luis, and that was when Sutton saw her dad. "Oh, Sutton, honey!" He burst out of the circle and crossed the parking lot like a bot on turbo speed.

Luis's mom was right behind him. "Luis!" she cried. "What happened?"

"Dad, I'm fine," Sutton said as he crushed her to him, her voice muffled and her face smooshed into her dad's jacket. She inhaled the wonderful, familiar scent of him. And then she was crying, and she didn't even know why, because they were finally here, together. Now that they were safe and she didn't have to be brave anymore, it all came flooding over her, and all she wanted was to be tucked up in their apartment with a cup of golden milk and Moti sleeping on her feet.

"Are you okay, honey?" Elizabeth's hand was soft on Sutton's head, stroking her hair. "We're so very, very sorry."

Sutton emerged from her dad's jacket to nod at Elizabeth, who had Luis firmly tucked under her arm. "I'm okay now."

"We walked to where we thought the tunnel would open out," Sutton's dad said. "But we couldn't find an opening."

Elizabeth rested her hand on his arm. "We kept walking, thinking maybe the tunnel dumped out farther along the trail. But it didn't."

"So eventually we doubled back and tried to go through the tunnel ourselves," Sutton's dad said as Elizabeth started to giggle, "but we didn't fit."

"Didn't fit?" she laughed. "You got stuck! I almost called the park ranger then!"

"We almost got stuck too," Luis said. "But Sutton helped me get out."

Their parents exchanged meaningful looks. "You guys worked together, huh?" Sutton's dad said.

Part of Sutton wanted to deny it. But they really had. Without Luis, she would probably still be sitting in that clearing, or she'd be stuck on the other side of that rickety bridge. Without Sutton, Luis could have been stung by a bee!

"Yeah," Luis said. "And we made it back to the parking lot."

"And so did we," his mom said.

"Because we made an emergency plan," Luis said.

"Yes, love," Elizabeth said.

There was a lot of explaining to the rangers and the officers how they'd gotten separated. Sutton showed the rangers on the old, faded map where the tunnel opened up, and they promised to block it over so no other kids would be lured in by the fantastical possibilities.

"We're so sorry," Martin said after the park rangers had gotten their statements and the search party had dispersed. "I was so sure the tunnel would open up farther along the main trail. When it didn't . . ."

"It was scary," Luis said. "But we had each other."

Sutton's dad wouldn't let go of her. She didn't really mind. "You guys must be starving," he said. "Do you want to go grab something to eat? There's a vegan place near here with good options for you, Luis."

Sutton didn't want to hurt Luis's feelings, but she was exhausted. One look and she could tell he felt the same way.

"No," they said together. "But thanks."

Sutton dug her watch out from under the driver's seat as soon as she got in the car. She strapped it on. Having a GPS unit next to her skin calmed her. Technology was her friend.

Sutton's dad and Luis's mom stood between the two cars, saying their goodbyes. Sutton looked away as her dad pressed a quick kiss to Elizabeth's lips.

The idea of them kissing wasn't as bad as it had been this morning. But that didn't mean she wanted to look at it.

"Oh, honey," he said when he got in the car. "Are you all right? You look pretty banged up."

"I just want to go home," she said.

His face fell as he pulled out of the lot. "I guess this was kind of a disaster. We're zero for two now."

"Actually, Dad"—his eyes lit up as he looked at her in the rearview mirror—"Luis wasn't that bad. Maybe we could ask him and Elizabeth to come over for our next movie night."

"Really?"

"Yeah. I didn't get to know Elizabeth at all."

"Thanks, pumpkin. That means so much to me that you're willing to try."

Sutton fiddled with the buttons on her GPS watch. "I'm always willing to try for you, Dad. But promise me one thing."

"Anything."

"No more hiking?"

He guffawed so loud, Luis and his mom probably heard him in the car behind them. "I promise. Absolutely no more hiking."

CHAPTER TWENTY-SIX

Luis

Luis was finishing up the crucial scene where the Whitlow School students freed their Alistair Academy rivals from the control of the Dark Force, when his mom stuck her head into his room.

"Sawyer will be here any minute," she said. "Can you come clear the table off? Your stuff is still spread out."

Luis tucked his notebook carefully into its drawer and headed out to the kitchen. His mom was preparing ingredients for personal pizzas, and she needed room to set all the different toppings out on the table so he and Sawyer could each make their own.

Luis had been sure Sawyer wouldn't want to hang out with him again after the guinea pig incident, but now he was coming over and Luis wanted everything to be perfect. They'd even bought real dairy cheese for Sawyer's pizza.

"Did you make any progress with that last night?" Luis's mom asked from the counter, where she was slicing bell peppers. The night before, she had gone to her room to do yoga and call Martin while Luis had stayed up to try to master the basics of mini-robots.

Now that Luis was almost done with Penelope Bell's story, he was starting to think about the next one he'd write. He thought it might be about robots, so he needed to learn the basics. First he'd talked to Sutton, but she'd gotten exasperated with his insistence on giving the robots personalities and opinions.

"The whole point is that they don't think! You program them to do what you want!" she said.

She had gotten so frustrated, she sent him home with one of her most basic mini-bots and some links on how to program it to move. "You need to see for yourself!" she'd said. "It doesn't matter how they *feel!*" She'd giggled when Luis insisted on naming the robot Bumble, but had strictly prohibited him from painting black and yellow stripes on it.

He could work on getting in touch with Bumble's feelings later.

"Not much progress," he admitted to his mom. "Though I did decide that Bumble's parents are named Honey and Digger."

She laughed and passed the bowls of cheese and tomato sauce across the counter for Luis to put on the table. "Somehow I don't think Sutton would approve of the bot having parents."

"Then she's really not going to approve of Bumble's dreams of becoming a country music star." Luis carefully tucked Bumble into the bot carrying case and set it on the highest bookshelf he could reach.

"You can tell her all about it tomorrow. What time are we supposed to be there?"

"Five." Luis had read Sutton's text inviting them to her not-birthday so many times that he'd memorized it. "But we still need to get a present!"

"I thought she said no presents."

"She said no birthday presents. She never said no not-birthday presents."

Luis's mom grinned and brought a few more toppings around to put on the table. "At first I thought you two might be too different to ever get along. Now I'm thinking you're more alike than anyone ever imagined!"

Luis glanced at the clock. Sawyer and his mom should have arrived by now.

"They're coming," his mom said, reading his mind. "If I recall correctly from when we served on the fall carnival committee together, Sawyer's mom has a tendency to run late."

If Luis recalled correctly, Sawyer's mom did not mind breaking a few traffic laws when she was really in a hurry. But hopefully his mom was right. It was a lot more comforting to blame Mrs. Lawson than to imagine Sawyer was having second thoughts about hanging out with him.

"And anyway, this gives me a minute to talk to you about something." His mom grabbed some papers from the counter and led him to the couch. "I know the hike was kind of a disaster"—Luis opened his mouth to object, but his mom went on before he could—"but you did an amazing job handling the challenges that arose, even when I wasn't there with you like I should have been."

"Sutton helped."

"I'm so glad she did. No matter where you go or what you do, there will always be people around to ask for help. Unless you decide to go climb Mount Rainier all by yourself, but that seems unlikely."

Luis snorted. He would leave the extreme adventure activities to Penelope Bell and her friends.

"I did a little digging." She laid a brochure on the couch between them. It said *The Greater Seattle Bureau of Fearless Ideas*. "They have writing workshops for kids and post some of the kids' work online. They even publish books with collections of kids' writing. I thought you might like to check it out."

Luis ran a hand over the brochure, almost afraid to pick it up. Maybe it would vanish in a puff of smoke. It seemed impossible. "Writing workshops? With other kids?"

"And . . . ," she went on. There was more? "The bookstore in the university district has a regular graphic novel club, where kids talk about their favorite graphic novels, and also learn about writing them. I was thinking about your dad's comics. . . ."

Suddenly Luis could think of nothing else. His dad's art, Luis's love of stories. Luis might not be the best artist in the world, but he could learn. Or he could partner up with someone who liked to draw but wanted someone else to come up with the story. The world seemed full of opportunity.

"Yes!"

His mom laughed. "You don't want to know more—"

"Yes!" Luis said. "I mean, no! I don't need to know more. I want to do them. Both of them. Can I do both?"

She took her face in his hands. "You can do both. You can do anything. Your papi would be so proud of you, Luisito."

A car door slammed outside, and they broke apart. "Sounds like Sawyer's here!" Mom said. "Shall we make some pizzas?"

CHAPTER TWENTY-SEVEN

Sutton

It was Sutton's birthday, but not.

Her mom's flight from the research station to Seattle (or really: from Antarctica to Christchurch, New Zealand; to Sydney, Australia; to Los Angeles; to Seattle) would get in a week after Sutton's actual birthday. So the plan was to wait and do their traditional family birthday celebration a few days late, when her mom could be there with them.

It wasn't what Sutton would have chosen, if she could have. But she wouldn't have chosen to get lost in the woods, get stung by a bee, land in a stream, and cross a structurally unsound bridge, either, and that had turned out all right. Finding her way back to her dad in the parking lot had made everything okay. If staying another week at the research station meant her mom got that much closer to saving the penguins, that was okay, too.

But her dad had said he couldn't possibly ignore the most important day of the whole year, the day that marked the birth of his brilliant daughter, so they'd decided to have an informal, totally-not-official, not-birthday birthday get-together.

Mrs. Banerjee's knee was miraculously healed by the prospect of cooking for a crowd, and she sent Sutton as her gofer between the apartments all day, since she had things baking in the ovens in both her apartment and theirs.

"It's not supposed to be a big deal," Sutton protested, when she saw how much work Mrs. B was doing.

"You think this is a big deal?" Mrs. B said with a laugh as she shredded carrots for the gajar ka halwa, a sweet Indian pudding Sutton had specifically requested. "You should have seen when my daughter got married. That was a big deal. This is a Sunday afternoon."

Everything smelled so good, Sutton wasn't going to protest too hard.

In her free moments between apartments, Sutton ran up the stairs to the rooftop patio, where her dad and Mr. Wong were dusting off the furniture and opening up the table umbrellas, in case the menacing thunderclouds made good on their threats. Moti and Freckles curled around each other on one of the cushioned benches.

"Does Freckles like the cat condo?" Sutton asked.

Mr. Wong beamed. "He does! So does Moti! Sometimes I think Mrs. Banerjee and I should break down the wall between our apartments so the animals can be together all the time."

Sutton grinned. She wasn't sure, but she thought Mr. Wong and Mrs. Banerjee would like that an awful lot too.

Dad's phone buzzed and he checked a text. "Sabina and Sadiq's soccer game just finished, so they should be here soon."

"Okay."

"And Riley and her family will be up as soon as the little one wakes from her nap."

Sutton nodded. Not so long ago, Riley felt like her fiercest rival. Sometimes she still would be, when they were vying for the top spot on their robotics team. But it didn't always have to be that way.

A couple of days after the hike, Sutton had knocked on Riley's door again. This time she was available to help, and together they figured out how to get the bot through the maze. Sutton had done almost all of it herself; she just needed a little bit of help with the last step, and that was okay. Now it would be ready to show her mom.

Her dad's phone buzzed again. "Oh! That's Liz. I'll go bring them up."

Sutton's stomach did a flip. It had been her choice to invite Luis and Elizabeth for her not-birthday birthday, but now that they were right downstairs, she felt a little nervous. They'd seen each other a couple of times in the weeks since the hike, but suddenly a family gathering like this one—even if it was a not-birthday—felt momentous.

What if they got along like cats and dogs, except regular cats and dogs, not like Freckles and Moti?

Which made Sutton realize: "Oh no! The animals have to go downstairs!" she said. "Luis is terrified of dogs!"

"Even Moti?" Mr. Wong looked at the little pile of fluff intertwined with Freckles on the bench.

Sutton thought about how Luis had reacted to the beautiful black Lab on the park trail. "I think it would be best."

"All right, dear." Mr. Wong hurried over to the animals and hoisted Freckles over his shoulder, knowing Moti would follow. "I'll be right back."

He disappeared into the stairwell, and Sutton was alone on the patio. But she wasn't alone, not really. So many people who loved her were bustling up and down the apartment building's stairs, preparing to not-celebrate her birthday.

The stairwell door swung open.

"Hi, Sutton." Luis stood there, holding a gift that looked like he'd wrapped it himself. "Happy not-birthday."

She beamed. If anyone would understand the concept of a not-birthday, it would be Luis.

"Thank you." Then she scowled. "But you weren't supposed to bring a present."

Since it was Sutton's not-birthday, she'd instructed her guests not to bring presents. All she wanted was their company—they wouldn't be a replacement for her mom, but they were the people who filled her life with love and fun, who guided her through the maze, even when Mom couldn't be there.

By opening herself up to Luis, and then to Riley, Sutton had finally achieved her goal. She'd been so focused on making the bot turn right to get through the maze exactly how she'd planned it. It turned out there was a different way. Just because coding was based in logical cause and effect didn't mean there was only ever one way to do something. In fact, there was almost always more than one way to arrive at a solution.

She and Luis had gotten through the park and back to where they belonged by a very different route than they'd planned. It had worked out. And who knew? If they'd stayed on the main path with their parents the whole way, things might have turned out very different. But now here they were, with Luis holding out a present.

"It's not a birthday present," Luis said, holding up the package, which was wrapped in Santa Claus wrapping paper. "See? No birthday paper." He set it on a table with a few other unauthorized presents.

Dad and Elizabeth came through the door next, and he held it open so Mrs. Banerjee could bustle through with a tray full of food. He took the tray from her, and then Mr. Wong appeared with two more trays, just as Aunt Lindsay arrived.

It took the adults one more trip back downstairs for plates and utensils, and then it was all laid out in front of them.

"This looks amazing," Elizabeth said. Mrs. Banerjee beamed. "Would you tell us about these dishes?"

Sutton knew that part of the question was whether or not Luis would be able to eat anything. Elizabeth had told them not to go to any trouble— they always traveled with special food for Luis. But when Sutton had told Mrs. Banerjee about Luis's allergies, she had taken it as a challenge.

"This," Mrs. B said, starting with a casserole dish full of what looked like mashed carrots, "is gajar ka halwa. A sweet dish that includes carrots, raisins, cardamom, coconut oil, and lots of sugar. It is normally made with cashews, but I left them out. And the milk has been replaced by rice milk. So I believe it should be a good choice for Luis."

Luis's eyes widened. He looked shocked that his food allergies had been considered.

She then went on to describe the two other Indian dishes—rasmalai, paneer balls in a sugary, creamy sauce; and jalebi, a sort of funnel cake soaked in saffron sugar syrup. She was careful to describe the allergens in each of them, but Luis had already started devouring the carrot dish with his eyes.

"And that one?" Mr. Wong said, pointing to the fourth dish.

"That," she said, with a twinkle in her eye, "is a traditional birthday dish going back many decades in my family. It is called Oreo pie."

The food kept everyone busy for a few minutes as they served themselves and found seats. Mrs. B kept up a cheerful stream of chatter, asking Elizabeth about her job, telling her all about Moti and Freckles, and asking pointed questions about how long Elizabeth and Sutton's dad had been dating.

Riley, her moms, and her little sister (wearing a tutu and construction helmet) arrived with more food and another not-birthday present. Finally Sabina and Sadiq were there too, sweaty in their soccer uniforms, but not too tired for a Ping-Pong tournament.

Luis and Sutton watched the twins take turns demolishing Riley in Ping-Pong for a bit, and then they drifted off to a bench a little ways away. "Thank you for inviting us," Luis said. "I hope your dad didn't make you."

Sutton flushed. She couldn't blame him for thinking that, but she wished he hadn't. "It was my idea."

"Oh! Well, thanks." Luis took a big bite of gajar ka halwa. "This is amazing," he mumbled around the sweet carrot mush.

Sutton had had gajar ka halwa before, so she started off with the jalebi and groaned as the sugar bomb exploded in her mouth.

Luis grabbed the smooshed not-birthday present off the nearby table. "Here. Open this."

Sutton took the package and turned it over curiously. Not that she'd expected a present at all, but if Luis was going to bring her something, she would have expected a book. This was way too small to be a book.

She set her plate aside and ripped into the package. "You really didn't have to bring me anything."

Luis shrugged. "You saved my life multiple times, so."

Sutton grinned. "I'd say we worked together to avoid dying in the wilderness of Discovery Park."

Inside the paper was another layer of tissue. She unwrapped and unwrapped and unwrapped. Luis had wrapped this package like it was about to go on a wilderness expedition. Finally her fingers found metal.

She pulled out what looked like an oversized silver locket at first. She fingered the cover, almost afraid to open it. She wasn't ready to find a photo of their parents inside, like Elizabeth was already her mom or something.

"Open it," Luis urged.

Sutton pried open the cover and found not a photo, but—

"A compass!" she laughed. "Wait, it's not your dad's, is it?"

Luis shook his head so fast it blurred. "No, no, my mom and I went to a bunch of Goodwills, looking for one that worked. This is the one we found for you. I know you have GPS and probably won't ever go hiking again, but . . ."

He suddenly looked nervous, like he'd made a big mistake.

Sutton looped the compass's chain around her neck. "I love it," she said. "Thank you. So I can always find my way home."

Luis sighed in relief. "Exactly."

She would always find her way home. She knew that now. Just like her mom would make it home, when the time was right. Even if she didn't take the route Sutton expected.

"Can I show you something?" Sutton retrieved her backpack from a corner.

"Isn't that your hiking backpack?" Luis eyed it warily.

Sutton grinned. "The only place I'm hiking is down to my apartment at the end of the night." She pulled out her mini-bot and the maze. "But I wanted you to see this."

She spread the maze out and calibrated her bot. "How's it going with the bot I loaned you?"

"Bumble? Buzzing right along." He grinned. "I mean, mostly he just goes in wonky circles. I think he's dancing."

Sutton rolled her eyes.

"What?" Luis laughed. "It's science. Bees share information with their bee friends through something called a waggle dance. I'm not even kidding."

Sutton fought to keep her own grin from showing through. "Who's the bot communicating with? You only have one."

"My guess is it's sending a signal to our robot overlords, who will soon seize all power from humans." Luis shrugged. "But what do I know?"

"Well, I'm still overlord of this bot." Sutton pulled out her tablet and opened up the app she needed, telling it to run the bot's code. They watched as the tiny machine, powered by ones and zeroes and the brain of a now-ten-year-old girl, motored through the maze. When it reached the spot where it had been getting stuck, Sutton watched the bot turn and go its own way.

It would still reach the other side.

The grown-ups had drifted over, drawn to the technology none of them understood. (Mrs. B understood the fundamentals, but when she'd taught computer science, a single computer had been the size of Sutton's bedroom, so it was understandable that she marveled over the tiny bot.)

When the bot reached the exit, they cheered. Sutton picked it up and started it at the beginning of the maze again. This time, instead of turning left at the tricky spot, the bot went straight.

"That's not what it did the last time!" Luis said.

Sutton nodded. "I found a bunch of different ways for it to get through. I decided instead of focusing on speed, I'd focus on possibilities. Eventually I want to teach it to choose the best route, depending on changing variables."

The variables might change sometimes, and the bot could learn to adapt. So could Sutton. She'd already started.

Just sitting here under the hazy Seattle sky, the same sky as the one a world away where Sutton's mom was tracking penguin migration, she was adapting. She was forging new paths.

She reached up and closed her fingers around the compass resting against her heart.

She was home.

ACKNOWLEDGMENTS

The idea for this book was first sparked when my father made a funny comment about being lost in a park. (We weren't as lost as Luis and Sutton, but like them, we couldn't find the parking lot.) At first I thought the story would be a picture book. But it wasn't. Then I thought it might be a chapter book. It wasn't.

That's when my lovely editor Reka Simonsen saw the potential for the middle-grade novel it became. Many thanks to Reka, my cartographer, for seeing what Luis and Sutton could be and providing the map to get them there. Thanks also to her wonderful assistant, Julia McCarthy, for carrying the first aid kit (aka providing insight and support as needed).

My agent, Jim McCarthy (no relation to Julia!), is my compass through the publishing wilderness. I don't think he would be a lot of help in an actual wilderness, but that's okay, because I'm staying inside with my computer, where I can email him at any moment with frantic questions.

A serious explorer doesn't mount an expedition without the support of many specialists. Publishing a book is sort of like mounting an expedition, but with a lot less potential for freezing or starvation. I am so grateful to these people at Atheneum and Simon & Schuster for making this book everything it could be: senior managing editor Jeannie Ng, copy editor Clare McGlade, designers Greg Stadnyk and Irene Metaxatos, and publicist Audrey Gibbons. And a million thank-yous to the incomparable Isabel Roxas for the most perfect cover.

My writing friends are my cairns along the way, but a lot warmer and more encouraging than a pile of rocks. Many thanks to the following people for their critiques, insights, support, and answers to my many questions about allergies, biracial identity, Indian food and culture, and more: Jessica Lawson, Rajani LaRocca, Alexandra Alessandri, Shanna Rogers, Summer Heacock, Ann Braden, and Tara Dairman.

Finally, my husband, Mariño, and my children, Joaquin and Cordelia, are my true North; I will always make my way back to you. (It helps that I almost never leave the house.)

TURN THE PAGE FOR A SNEAK PEEK AT
ACROSS THE POND.

Callie pressed her forehead to the thick windowpane and looked out across the rolling hills. She wanted to drink in everything at once—the infinite shades of green, the mossy stone walls along winding paths, the sheep grazing in far-off fields. A draft danced across the back of her neck, but the chill was quickly replaced by a flicker of something Callie hadn't felt in ages. Maybe ever.

Possibility.

At home, her life was small. Small apartment, small people. Making herself smaller and smaller until she almost disappeared.

But here, in an actual castle where everything was

larger than any life she'd ever known, where the grassy fields beyond the window stretched out like an ocean of green, she already felt her world expanding.

She felt her *self* expanding.

Callie wasn't the kind of girl who traveled to Europe, like Kate, who "wintered" in Switzerland, or Imogen, who spent her birthday in Paris. The only place Callie had ever traveled was Phoenix. It was sadly lacking in magical fire-birds.

But now here she was. In Scotland. In an actual castle.

Even the exhaustion of the endless travel from San Diego to New York to London to Edinburgh to the village of South Kingsferry couldn't extinguish the new thing bubbling up inside her.

"Hey kiddo," her dad said, peeking his head into the billiards room. "Are you joining us for the rest of the tour?"

Of course she was. Callie wanted to turn over every stone in this fortress of a place, from the servants' quarters to the castle keep, an enormous tower at the castle's center. For hundreds of years, the keep had been a lookout to watch for enemies and take refuge if the worst should happen.

"Where's the moat?" Callie's little brother, Jax, had asked when they first arrived. Their parents had laughed.

It wasn't such a silly question, though. Some of Callie's

daydreams in the months leading up to the trip definitely included moats. But her parents had been here before. To them it was less of a fantasy.

"No moat," Dad said. "Or drawbridge. It wasn't the sort of castle with its own military. Just a family and their servants. And visiting nobles."

Generations upon generations of an old Scottish family named Spence had lived and died in this place, and in between they'd had dreams and fears and great loves and crushing disappointments. Even when the Spence line had dwindled down to only Lady Philippa Whittington-Spence, she'd made sure to keep it a place where a family could build something together, safe from intruders.

"Where'd you run off to?" Mom asked, when Dad appeared with Callie in tow.

"I found her in the billiards room," Dad said.

"Billiards?!" Jax screeched, appearing from behind a massive gold chair. "I wanna see!"

He took off running and Dad sprinted after him.

"What do you think?" Mom asked, staring at the massive portrait of a stern man in a military uniform, hanging over the biggest fireplace Callie had ever seen. "I always felt like this guy was judging me."

"Is it all the same?" Callie asked. "From when you lived here before?

"Pretty much. All your first impressions . . . I bet

they're the same as mine the first time I arrived. Almost twenty years ago now!"

"You're old," Callie said, and Mom laughed.

"What do you think? You okay?"

Callie nodded. She was more than okay. "I guess I can't quite believe this is really happening. I mean . . . we *live* here now."